Temptation . . .

I stared at Lou unabashedly while he worked. He was wearing a fitted white T-shirt, and those muscles he worked so hard on were now hard at work. His biceps pulled and wrenched, straining the sleeves of his shirt. Then I looked down at his legs, which were bent into a squatting position. Under his jeans they looked nicely shaped and strong.

Suddenly an image of Scott popped into my mind—tall, slender, strong. But strong in a different way—maybe an inferior way, some traitorous part of my mind suggested. I squashed the thought and tore my gaze away from Lou's incredible body to stare at the ice plant along the highway. It wasn't much to look at, but I had to stare at something other than the guy my best friend was after.

Read these other romances from
HarperPaperbacks

My Phantom Love
Looking Out for Lacey
The Unbelievable Truth
Runaway
Cinderella Summer
Wild Hearts
Can't Buy Me Love
Choose Me
My Sister's Boyfriend
On My Own

And don't miss

Freshman Dorm—the Hit Series!
by Linda A. Cooney

Now twenty-three titles strong!

My Cheating Heart

Ann Steinke

HarperPaperbacks

A Divison of HarperCollins*Publishers*

This is a work of fiction. The characters, incidents, and dialogues are products of the author's imagination and are not to be construed as real. Any resemblance to actual events or persons, living or dead, is entirely coincidental.

HarperPaperbacks   *A Division of* HarperCollins*Publishers*
10 East 53rd Street, New York, N.Y. 10022

Produced by Daniel Weiss Associates, Inc.
33 West 17th Street, New York, New York 10011.

First printing: January, 1993

Printed in the United States of America

HarperPaperbacks and colophon are trademarks of HarperCollins*Publishers*

10 9 8 7 6 5 4 3 2 1

My
Cheating
Heart

one

"I am so mad!" Teresa Martinez said, standing across the counter from me in Taco Bell. She'd come a little early to pick me up from work at the end of my shift. "I am so—" She took deep breaths, her hands clenched into fists at her sides. Her posture was ramrod straight, and her dark eyes looked as if they could shoot sparks.

"Ter! What happened?" I asked, casting a quick look around to see if Ernesto, my manager, was on the prowl. There was no sign of him, so I turned my attention back to my best friend.

"I am so mad I—" She heaved another chest-deep sigh. Ter tends to get emotional about a lot of things, so it was difficult for me to figure

1

out if this was just another one of her over-dramatic reactions to something. I was sure I'd find out as soon as I got off work, though.

"I'm gonna murder someone!" she ranted.

"Ter—" I began. She was really letting herself get carried away this time.

"No, with my luck I'd get caught," she went on as if she didn't hear me.

"Teresa Martinez!" I exclaimed, finally grabbing her attention. I wanted to laugh, but instead I turned toward the drink machine and filled a paper cup with ice and Coke. Shoving it at her, I said, "Here. Go have a Coke and calm down."

She made a batting motion with her hand in dismissal. "I'm not calming down. Besides, there's caffeine in Coke and that won't calm me down." Her face was flushed, and her mouth turned down in a pout.

I shook my head, and my long, straight blond hair rippled down my back. It was slipping out of the job-required ponytail. "7-up then," I said. Placing the Coke off to the side, I prepared a cup of the clear drink and shoved it at Teresa. "Ter, just wait until I'm off work to have your nervous breakdown, okay?"

"I don't want to wait!" Teresa wailed. "But I guess I have to." She made a frustrated noise deep in her throat, grabbed the drink, and said, "Go back to work. Don't mind me. I'll wait in the corner. And by the way, I think there's caffeine in 7-up, too."

With her dark hair flying wildly, Ter flounced over to the booth farthest from the front entrance, and slid in. An old-fashioned lamp hung directly over her, casting the contours of her face in light and shadow. She reminded me of one of those charcoal drawings we used to try to do in art class. The effect showed how pretty she was. I flashed her a smile, and Ter raised her cup in mock salute. Then I promptly turned to wait on the next customer before Ernesto had a chance to say something like, "You're not paid to chat with your friends, Miss Stevens."

The sleepy atmosphere of Taco Bell was made even more so by the darkness outside. Soon it would be ten o'clock, and I could get off work. I was exhausted, and as much as I loved my best friend, I wasn't sure I had the energy to deal with her latest crisis—whatever it was. But I knew I owed Ter my full attention. After all, she had been driving me to and from work for weeks, ever since my car had broken down.

At ten sharp, Teresa appeared like magic across the counter from me. "Come on, you gringo. Let's get out of here," she said, her words full of barely suppressed laughter.

Teresa thinks it's a real joke that I—blond and blue-eyed—work in a Mexican fast-food

3

restaurant. She works in a shop in San Luis Obispo, selling dried flowers, both loose and in arrangements, and she often jokes that we have our jobs mixed up. "You should be downtown in SLO, and I should be out here, tossing tortillas," she says. And I always point out that she's stereotyping. "Remember what my mother's always preaching," I tell her, and Ter nods and joins in chanting with me, "Don't lump people together." Then we grin at each other, and she sighs and says, "You're right." But then, the next time, she does it all over again.

I collected my purse, then joined Teresa out front. We exited the small building and stepped into the cool night. I followed Teresa to her battered old Chevy Malibu and sat next to her in the front seat.

"So, what's up?" I asked.

"I want you to be the first to know," Ter said seriously. "I'm done with guys. I'm through with the suckers. . . . Hey! This is serious. It's not funny. Why are you laughing?"

My chest hurt as I struggled to stifle my laughter. "Oh, Ter! You must say that six times a month. What happened?"

"That creep Carlos. I practically poured my lifeblood out for him, helping him with his English essay for summer school. You should have heard the way he pulled on my heartstrings, with this business about how he'd get axed from the football team this year if he didn't pass English. He had to do really well on his essay, so I—like a dope—wrote practically the whole thing for him. That louse took it from me like that—" She snapped her fingers to illustrate. "Then he never spoke to me again."

I tried to think of something suitably comforting to say, but Ter went on before I had a chance to get a word in.

"I saw him today when he and a bunch of his buddies were out cruising on Higuera Street. So I asked how he did. 'Oh,' he said. 'I passed. Did great. Got a *C* in the class. A *C,* mind you! Big deal. So I asked him about the essay. 'Yeah, that was great. I got a *B*+ on that.' He got the *B*+! I wrote the thing! And did I get any credit? No. Did he ever say thanks? No! I'm so mad at that creep. . . ."

I let Teresa mutter on, but as she did, I reached over, took her keys out of her purse, and put them in the ignition. Then I started the car and pointed it down the street. Without missing a beat Teresa put the car in gear, and the thing lurched forward and moved fairly smoothly out of the parking lot onto Olive Street.

". . . and I tell you, he must have told his buddies all about me, because I swear they were

5

laughing at me! So that's it. I don't care if the next guy that comes along looks like he's straight out of Hollywood, I'm not gonna be impressed. And I'm gonna seriously look into becoming a nun!" Teresa took a breath and looked at me. "I mean it," she said decisively.

"Sure," I said. "Look, I have to pick up some milk for Mom on the way home, okay?"

Teresa shook her head, making her heavy brown hair fan out over her shoulders. Her dark eyes snapped in anger. "You don't believe me," she said, throwing me an accusing look. "Why don't you believe me?" She wrenched the wheel sharply, and we flew around the corner, following the signs for Highway 101.

I tried to stabilize myself by holding on to the door handle more tightly. "Because you've said you're done with guys too many times before," I answered. "You said that after you broke up with Chris Ortega, and after Daniel Lopez left you for that out-of-town girl, and . . ."

"Okay, okay! Shut up," Ter said, but I heard a hint of laughter in her voice. She screeched down the ramp and whipped onto the southbound lane of 101. Then she started muttering again. "Maybe that rat would have been nicer to me if I'd lost some weight."

"Ter! You're fine. You're gorgeous!" I said, launching into my familiar counterargument.

Physically, Ter and I are opposites. She has a figure that can be called lush, while I'm built more on the line of a drinking straw. And we had contrasting personalities, too. One of our ninth-grade teachers once said, "You are two of the most unlikely friends I'd ever hope to see." But why should differences rule out friendships? I had argued. Why couldn't differences make a friendship richer and more interesting? I never look at our differences as divisive factors. I look at them as comic relief—a never-ending source of amusement.

I think it's funny, for example, the way Teresa uses as a mirror any surface smooth enough to reflect her image. She's forever checking to see if she looks okay. Is her hair wild and all over the place, or just right? Is her mascara running or flaking off? Is her lipstick smeared? Do her clothes make her look fat?

I, on the other hand, can walk by rows of cosmetic counters and never pause to look at myself. And I stopped wearing lipstick to school a long time ago because I always eat it off by the end of second period anyway. And my hair is perfectly straight, so there's nothing I need to check in a mirror. But Teresa can't even walk in a straight line if she sees something shiny off to the side.

The glare of the headlights from an

approaching car illuminated the masses of almost-black hair fluffing out behind Teresa's head. Teresa has hair that can be weighed in pounds. I have hair that can be weighed in ounces. "You want to lose weight?" I said jokingly. "Get a haircut."

Teresa groaned out loud. "Is it really that bad? Do I need a cut?"

"Oh, Ter!" I lamented. I should never have made a joke about her hair. I know how she takes everything to heart.

We were approaching the city limits of Pismo Beach. In the fog, all the street lights seemed to have halos around them. It's often cool and foggy at night on the California central coast. The sun might shine all day long, but when it finally sets, the air becomes cool, and the fog rolls in from its parking spot on the ocean.

"Take the Marsh exit," I instructed Ter. "I'll grab Mom's milk."

She roared down the off ramp, brought the car to a barely civilized semistop, and zipped down the main drag. Teresa's driving was on the wild side, so I always rode with my feet securely planted underneath the dashboard, and my left arm crossed over my chest so that I can hang on to the door handle with both hands. Two seconds later, I pointed to a spot on the curb in front of the Quick Stop convenience store. "Pull

8

over there, and I'll just jump out and run in," I told her.

"No way," she replied. "It's late at night. I'll go with you. You could get mugged out there all by yourself."

"Ter, we could *both* get mugged."

"Yeah, but it wouldn't be so easy. One of us could always hit the assailant over the head with my purse."

"All right, Teresa. You win," I said, laughing. I wouldn't have been able to stop her anyway. And she was probably right about that purse. Since it seemed to contain her entire cosmetics collection, along with a zillion other things she thinks she's going to need, it weighed a ton. Still, Ter's only five four, and I wasn't sure she actually had the strength to use that purse as a weapon.

The Quick Stop was one of those small but incredibly packed stores where things are stacked literally to the ceiling. The off-white floors gleamed underfoot. The glass doors of the refrigerated sections were smudgeless. Whoever was in charge of the store obviously had high standards. As I entered the store, Ter grabbed my wrist, pulling me to an abrupt halt.

"What's the matter?" I asked, turning toward her.

"Oh, why didn't I take off those five pounds I

was gonna lose before school began?" she grumbled. She fluffed out her pounds of hair, then tugged at her blouse.

"Ter, the aisles aren't that narrow," I teased and tried to move on. Ter's fingers clutched my arm tighter.

"Look at those two hunks," she said, pulling me closer.

I followed her line of vision. There were two guys down the aisle from us. One obviously worked there, because he was taking things out of a large carton and setting them on a shelf. The other, a tall sandy-haired guy, was slouched against the shelving unit, talking to his friend. Whatever he was saying must have been funny, because although the dark-haired guy was facing away from us, I could see his shoulders shaking from laughter.

"Those are the guys for us," Teresa whispered. "The dark one's mine. You can have the Nordic type."

"Yeah? And what if I want the dark one?" I said just to tease. Ter frowned at me as though she wasn't sure if I was being serious. I grinned and shook a finger at her. "There you go, lumping again," I said in a scolding tone.

"Hhhh," she grunted, grabbing at my finger. "Well, you have to admit. You and the tall one kind of look alike. You'd make a nice couple."

10

Now I was getting irritated. "Ter, what has looking alike got to do with it? You and I are great friends, and we don't look anything like each other. In fact, being from different backgrounds is kind of neat."

Ter just shrugged and grinned. "Don't lecture me. Just let me gaze at him!" she said, turning to do just that.

"Ter, you really are impossible!" I said, forcefully pulling her with me over to the dairy section. "You just got through telling me that you're going to be a nun."

"But that was before I saw that great-looking guy."

"Yeah, and you said it wouldn't matter if you met someone straight out of Hollywood," I reminded her. I reached over and snagged a carton of skim milk from the shelf, all the while holding on to her wrist.

Teresa craned her neck around to see the two guys, and squirmed to release herself from my grip. "When did you decide to take what I say seriously?" she asked, successfully pulling away from me. She positioned herself a little closer to the guys, and a deep sigh of appreciation escaped her lips. "Besides, he's better than anything out of Hollywood." I came over and snatched her away from the scene.

"How do you know he's great-looking?" I

objected. "He was turned the other way."

"Buns. Great buns," Teresa said, ignoring the groan rising deep in my throat. "I wonder what his name is. I know I've seen those buns before."

I rolled my eyes and tucked the carton of milk under an arm. "I don't know how I ended up with such a boy-crazy friend," I teased.

"And I don't know how I ended up with one who's unconscious," Teresa returned.

I headed toward the checkout counter, dragging Teresa along with me. As we passed the end of the aisle where we had seen the two guys, we both paused to look. Now the one with dark hair was turned more toward us. We could see his profile and the full-face view of the blond guy. Both guys were good-looking. The blonde looked a good four to five inches taller than his friend. The dark-haired one looked Chicano, like Teresa, although he had a narrower face than most of the Mexican-Americans I know. Maybe he wasn't all Mexican.

"Come on," I urged. "Those two look like the types who have strings of girls hanging on them. And I have to get home. Tomorrow's the first day of school, and I'm beat."

"You're right. I'll bet they're just like Carlos," Teresa said in a rare moment of clear thinking. "I gotta listen to myself."

"Right," I said. "From now on, every time you look at a guy, just keep saying 'Carlos, Carlos' over and over again, like a chant. It'll keep you out of trouble." I paid the man behind the counter for the milk. He was Chicano, like the guy stocking shelves.

He smiled at us. "Have a good night, girls."

"Thanks." I smiled back, and then towed Teresa, who was entertaining second thoughts about giving up men, out of the store and over to her car, where I practically stuffed her behind the steering wheel.

"Come on, you flirt," I said indulgently. "Let's get home. We need our sleep if we're going to face the first day of our senior year tomorrow."

"Flirt!" Teresa objected, scandalized. Then the second part of my speech seemed to sink in. "Senior year," Ter echoed. "Only one more year, and we'll get sprung from prison! I can't wait."

I just smiled at her and sighed, laying my head against the top of the seat back. Ter had to be one of the most resilient, positive people I knew. She hadn't had it easy with guys in the past, but she quickly got over the bad experiences to seek out the good ones. I thought about how rotten Chris and Daniel had treated her. She had entered those relationships so trustingly, but neither of the guys had really been serious about dating her. In fact, both had dated other girls at the same time without telling her. And Ter always seemed to throw herself into relationships with her whole heart, sometimes forgetting to use her head.

I sat up and looked at Ter. "Listen, Ter," I said earnestly. "Someday a guy's going to walk into your life, and he'll be the one. He'll like you for who you are—not how he can use you. He'll be better than all the guys who've hurt you in the past. He'll make you forget all about them. I just know it."

For once, Teresa didn't argue. Maybe she wanted to believe me so much that she was shoving down any thoughts she might have had about the likelihood of my prophecy.

My own experience with boys has been pretty run of the mill. I've dated about four guys since ninth grade, but none of them made me fall madly in love. They were nice; just not special. Ter thinks it's because I have perfectionist tendencies. Well, maybe I do, but at least I haven't been hurt like she has.

Fifteen minutes later, Teresa and I were pulling up to my house in the nice section of a town below Pismo Beach. My father's a contractor, and he built our house. The concrete drive curves in an arch and passes beneath a portico that protects the entryway to the house. It had just started to rain, so I was grateful for the shelter as I got ready to dash inside. "Thanks for the ride," I said.

Teresa shrugged. "No problem. When's your car gonna get fixed?" she asked, shifting her eyes toward my Toyota Tercel parked off to the side of the driveway.

I glanced at the car. "When I've saved enough," I said with a sigh. "Maybe next month."

"Well, don't worry about it," Ter said. "You know I'll take you to work and pick you up anytime."

"You're the best, Ter," I said fondly.

"Aren't I?" Ter said cockily, and we both laughed.

I swung open the door and clutched the carton of milk close to my body. "See you bright and early," I said with exaggerated cheerfulness.

Ter groaned. "Yeah. Six thirty. Ugh!"

Smiling at her, I got out of the car, then ducked my head back in. "And *don't* forget your violin," I told her.

"I won't," Ter said, grinning at me unabashedly. It's no secret that Teresa can be a flake sometimes and forget important things, like her instrument for orchestra the next day. "I've got it right next to our front door," she assured me. "That way I can't forget it."

"Good thinking," I said with approval. I closed the door and ran up the steps to the house.

Warm light shone through the frosted oval window in the front door. I entered and immediately kicked off my shoes, leaving them on the sisal mat in the hallway.

I found my father standing by the bay window in the living room, looking out. He smiled at me as I came over to join him. I love it when he's there to greet me when I come home. I love his face, and his round, happy expression. I love his crinkly gray eyes, and the way his salt-and-pepper hair waves back from his forehead. I don't look anything like him. But people say my mother and I could win a mother/daughter look-alike contest. Both of us are thin, blue-eyed, and blond—although my mother reluctantly admits to having to *encourage* her hair to remain blond these days.

"Raining," he commented unnecessarily.

"It's kind of a fine mist," I added.

"Yeah. I was just watching it," he said. "You know what it looks like?" I didn't answer. My father never pauses long enough so that anyone can. "It looks just like snow if you look at it in the light of the streetlamp."

"Snow?" I said, leaning over to peer out the window.

I had never seen snow until we moved to Washington State a couple of years back. There I'd seen it for the first time. It had been beautiful, especially against the backdrop of Puget Sound. I could still remember it so vividly—huge moist flakes, like glittering prisms from heaven.

But my mother hadn't thought the snow was so great. She ached for California. "I'm a Californian, born and bred," she'd say. "I have to go home." And my father would then break into song: "I left my heart in San Francisco," he'd sing, even though it wasn't in San Francisco that she'd left her heart. That drove my mother nuts.

We finally moved back to the central coast after two years, just this summer. At first I had been sorry to say good-bye to the trees, the mountains, the snow. . . . But then I realized that I'd also be coming back to Teresa, whom I've known since second grade. Even back then, we were great friends. And each year after that only intensified our friendship.

To me, Teresa is like light and life. She's so full of fun and warmth, and she makes up for everything I had to say good-bye to in Washington. Even though there were a couple of girls I grew to like in Washington, I hadn't been able to find a friend like Ter, and I knew I never would. My friendship with Teresa is so special that we've decided we're like the characters in the Bette Midler movie *Beaches*. Of course, neither one of us intends to die young. But our friendship won't die either. We've vowed to never let anything come between us.

I linked my arm through my father's and smiled. "Yeah, if you squint, it looks like snow," I agreed softly.

"Who's squinting?" he said, making me laugh.

"What are you two looking at?" my mother said, coming into the room behind us.

My father and I shared a secret smile. "Oh, nothing," he said, and we both turned away from the window. We knew my mother wouldn't share our memory of snow with similar fondness.

My mother raised one eyebrow and gave us one of her I-don't-believe-you-but-I'll-let-it-pass looks. Then she turned to me. "How was work?" she asked.

I shrugged. "Oh, you know. Workish." I don't like talking about work. Work is a necessity—not exactly an agreeable topic for conversation. "Well, I'd better get some sleep. Tomorrow's the first day of school," I said. "I can't believe it came so fast. Seems like we just moved back here. But that was two months ago."

"Yes, but it seems like we've always been here," my mother said with deep satisfaction.

"That's because we have," Dad put in dryly.

When the building business on the central coast had become a little tight, my family had moved up north because supposedly things were better up there. As it turned out, business was better there, but the difference wasn't enough to offset Mom's homesickness. Then things started to pick up again in California. Fortunately my father had left his partner in charge at home, so all he had to do was move his base of operations back. We moved back into our house, which we'd rented while we were gone, but business in California isn't *so* great that my parents, who both work, can buy me anything I want. "Only the have-tos," they like to say, which is why I have to work.

I gave Mom a peck on the cheek and hugged Dad. "See you in the morning," I said and headed for my room.

two

"It just never works out," I said to Ter the next morning on our way to school. I had assumed my usual traveling position in her car—feet firmly planted against the underside of the dashboard, left arm across my body, a white-knuckle grip on the door handle. My head was pressed against the seat back for stability, and the position was excellent for looking out the windows at the landscape.

"What never works out?" Ter asked, braking at a stop sign just barely long enough to be considered legal.

I turned to look at her. "Have you ever noticed that when you have to go somewhere awful—like to the dentist for a filling—and you

20

want the weather to match your mood, it never cooperates?"

I saw her mouth turn up at the corners. "Yeah, I'll bet there's some unwritten law about that," she said. A pedestrian stepped off the curb and Ter slammed on the brakes. My head snapped back, and I stared out the window while we waited for the person to get across. Then Ter accelerated and looked at me. "So?"

"So today's a gorgeous day," I said, pointing out the window. "And we're on our way to *school*." It was one of those days my grandmother calls "wine and roses" days. I'm not sure why that description is supposed to be appropriate, but despite my lack of understanding, I couldn't get that phrase out of my mind on a day like today. The sky was so blue, it hurt to look at it. The ocean seemed close enough to touch. It somehow seemed unfair that on such a day, we had to return to school.

"It should have been raining today," I said. "Or at least foggy. I don't feel like going to school."

"I hear you, but at least you'll get to see everyone you haven't seen since you got back," Ter pointed out.

"I've seen almost everyone at Taco Bell. And Jojo and Cathy have stopped by lots of times," I said. "Anyway, I think there should be a policy that school is never held on good-weather days, only bad-weather ones." I'm not against school on an intellectual level. I actually appreciate the value of learning and I get mostly As. But I'd much rather learn at home, on my own time. Say, after I've spent the whole day doing something fun, like going to the beach or shopping. "To have to spend a beautiful day like this one cooped up in classrooms is criminal," I concluded.

"I agree," Ter said, nodding. "We should go driving on the beach. . . ." Her voice trailed off and she scowled. "But there's no one to do it with, anyway." She meant no guys, and her disgust at this realization was made evident by the level of malice with which she negotiated a turn onto Elm. My right shoulder slammed into the door.

"Ouch!" I cried.

"I'm sorry," she apologized sincerely. I stifled a grin and rubbed my shoulder. Ter is impossible. Even on the first day of school, boys were uppermost in her mind. But at least that kept her from dwelling on the fact that we'd be spending the better part of a beautiful day trapped in classrooms.

We arrived at the school with depressing speed, and Ter parked the car in the student lot. Small clusters of kids were standing around in front of the main building, probably catching up on the latest news before the warning bell rang. As I scanned the crowd for anyone I might recognize, the diversity of the faces I saw suddenly struck me. One of the really nice things about returning to school on the central coast was that the student population was so mixed. Here there were caucasians, Chicanos, blacks, and Asians. I had missed that variety up north.

Ter and I got out of the car with the same eagerness of someone about to have a leg cut off. We'd already compared class schedules. Except for study hall and English, we had only orchestra at the end of the day in common. The warning bell rang.

"Good-bye!" Ter cried as if we were going to be parted forever.

"Good-bye!" I laughed, and we hugged. Kids flowed around us, and we joined the current, each heading her own way.

The last period of the day rolled around, and Ter and I were standing outside the door to orchestra with our violins in our arms.

"It's going to be so great having you back in orchestra with me," Ter said, hugging the case to her chest.

"I know. Now you'll have someone to keep

you on key," I teased.

Ter wrinkled her nose at me, then turned and entered the room first. I followed, but rammed right into her when she suddenly stopped short.

"Ter!" I yelled.

"Oh, you're not gonna believe it!" she said, squealing.

"What?"

"They're here," she breathed.

I squirmed around her and peered into the room, which was filling up with kids. But I saw nothing that should merit such excitement from her. "Who?" I asked. "Aliens from Mars?"

"No, you idiot," she answered. "Those two hunks from last night."

I looked where she was pointing and saw them. The dark-haired guy was sitting behind the drums as if he belonged there. The blonde stood next him. They were talking, and the blonde was looking around the room. As we stared at them like jerks, standing right inside the door, his gaze passed over us, then whipped back. He said something to his friend, and the dark-haired one looked in our direction too. That was when I glanced behind us to see who was standing there. I had expected to find two gorgeous girls waiting for us to get out of their way, but only Daniel

Nguyen was waiting there, looking annoyed. Dan had been first-chair violinist ever since I had joined orchestra, and he was probably disgusted that we were keeping him from getting to his seat. I pulled Ter off to the side, allowing Dan to stalk into the room.

"Come on, Ter. Let's get set up," I said, dragging her over to our assigned chairs in the violin section. We had looked up our seats on a chart outside the room. Ter and I were going to be sitting right next to each other, just like old times. As I made my way across the room, I tried not to look back at the two guys. The effort seemed superhuman.

Ter wasn't even trying not to look at them. Stumbling over a chair she didn't see, she said, "I can't believe those two are in orchestra. I can't believe it."

I pushed her down in her assigned seat and took my own. Opening my violin case, I said, "Ter, get a grip. Forget about them. I'll bet they've got girls who volunteer to do their laundry."

Ter shook her head, clearing it. "Yeah."

"Ter, just get your violin out. Tune it up," I instructed as if I were speaking to a particularly dull child. "And remember—Carlos."

"Yeah. Carlos, Carlos," she chanted.

Jojo Marsh, our conductor's daughter, and

Cathy Miller descended on us at that moment. Jojo bounced down the risers and reached up to hug me as if she hadn't seen me only three days before. Cathy trailed behind her, moving as slowly as ever. "Hi, guys!" I said, returning Jojo's hug.

Then Mr. Marsh began rapping his baton against the conductor's stand, and Jojo and Cathy immediately scampered back to their places. I looked at him and found that he looked exactly as he had two years before. He was frowning down at us as usual. He always frowns. Ter jokes that his facial muscles are permanently stuck in frown mode, and that if you sneak up on him while he's sleeping, you'd still find the same expression etched on his face. We once asked Jojo to test this theory about her father, but she just laughed. He tapped the podium with his baton one last time. "All right everyone, places, please."

It was several minutes before everyone had calmed down. Out of the corner of my eye, I watched the blond guy move from the drum section to the other side of the room. Then I noticed him pause near our one harp player and take a seat. He played the cello! I couldn't believe it. He didn't look like the cellist type. In fact, someone who looked like he did, the typical California surfer type, didn't seem to fit in orchestra at all. Well, life is full of surprises.

Mr. Marsh called for order once again, and I wrenched my mind from the fascinating subject of beach boys who play string instruments. During the next thirty minutes Mr. Marsh handed out music and discussed the year's program of concert dates. Then we practiced for the last fifteen minutes.

At the end of the period, Dan turned to me. The disgusted look that had been on his face at the beginning of the period had now assumed even greater intensity. "Everyone played as if they'd all had lobotomies over the summer," he commented.

"Well, we can't all be perfect like you, Dan," Ter chirped at him. She was joking, of course. I knew it.

But Dan didn't. He smiled in that superior way of his. "Yes," he said haughtily. "But it's obvious no one's even tried to keep up their practice over the summer." He rose, picking up his violin as if it were made of some precious substance, and put it in its case. I think he loves that violin more than any human being is supposed to love anything.

I turned away and began packing up my own instrument and collecting my music. Dan has always annoyed me beyond measure. Ter tells me again and again that the only way to deal with him is to ignore him, but Dan makes that impossible. His ego is so big, kids are constantly trying to deflate it. I'm sure it can't be done, but everyone keeps trying anyway.

Ter and I began threading our way toward the door, talking to Jojo and Cathy. We stepped through the door, and suddenly found our progress impeded by the two guys we'd been trying to pretend we hadn't noticed. The blonde stood in front of me; the dark one had Ter blocked.

Cathy gave a little cough. "Well, uh, we'll catch you guys later," she said, reaching out and snagging Jojo by the arm. Jojo winked at me before being pulled away, and while Ter and I watched the girls amble away, smiling over their shoulders, I prayed the guys hadn't noticed their silly behavior.

Up close I had a chance to really study them. The taller blond guy was dressed in a printed shirt and baggy gray pants. He had hazel eyes with laugh lines etched at the outside corners. The other guy wore blue jeans and a plain white T-shirt. His eyes exactly matched Ter's— a dark, fathomless brown.

"Hi," the blonde said, flashing a smile so perfect it could only be the result of braces. I'm always very conscious of people's teeth, because my eyeteeth are spun a quarter-turn. They look like fangs, but my dentist tells me the defect isn't enough to merit braces, since every other tooth in my mouth is fine. So I really envy people who had gotten braces.

"Hi," I said. Really, really intelligent dialogue, I thought.

Ter moved into action. "Hi. I don't think I remember you from orchestra last year," she said to the blonde. Then she smiled her beautiful smile at the dark-haired guy in front of her, and he returned it.

"I've been here," the dark-haired guy explained. "But Scott just rejoined orchestra this year after being out of it for a couple of years."

"Oh, yeah?" Ter said brightly. She nodded her head in my direction. "Then you have something in common with Krista. She's been out of town for two years."

Boy, talk about cut to the chase. Ter wasn't wasting any time.

Scott looked at me. "I'm Scott Hunter." He smiled, waiting.

"I'm Krista Stevens. "This is Teresa Martinez."

"Yeah, I remember," the other said, looking at Ter. "I've seen you in orchestra before. I'm Lou Pacheco. Drums."

"Right." Ter's glowing eyes advertised interest. "I kind of remember you," she said slowly, "but you seem to have changed somehow."

Lou looked a little uncomfortable, and a

lopsided grin spread across his face. "I used to wear glasses," he explained. "I've got contacts now. And I started working out with weights last year, trying to develop some muscles."

"Oh," Ter said, admiring the muscles under discussion. For some reason, her gaze only seemed to increase Lou's discomfort, which surprised me. I would have thought a guy who worked out would be glad to be admired.

"I noticed you play violins," Scott said, looking at me. "Must be tough playing next to our friend Dan."

I looked at him, realizing that he was at least five inches taller than me. Over six feet, I estimated. "Yeah," I said. "Sometimes his head gets in the way of my music, but I manage."

The guys laughed, then Scott turned to me again. "So where were you for two years?" he asked.

"I was in Seattle," I answered. "My family had to move there for business reasons, but my Mom missed this area so much, we finally moved back just this last July."

"Oh yeah?" he said, nodding. "So what are you, a junior or a senior?"

"We're seniors," I said. "You?"

"Yup. It's our last year, too, thank God," Scott said. "I have a feeling this is going to be a bummer of a year."

"Why's that?" I asked.

"Yeah, what's your problem?" Lou put in. "We're top of the heap this year."

Scott grinned. "There is that, but unfortunately, this is also the year I have to start seriously thinking about college and getting good scores on the SATs in October." He grimaced. "You'd think with two parents who were dropouts in the sixties, I'd get a break. But *no*. Somewhere along the line they got a social conscience, and now they think I'm supposed to make up for all the things they didn't do right—like take education seriously."

I laughed. "I know what you mean. My parents were sixties people too, but you'd never know it. We live like supernormal people," I said with suitable disgust.

"Well, at least I can't say *we* live like normal people," Scott said.

"No? Why's that?" I prompted.

"My dad runs the Surf City shop in Arroyo Village, and Mom's got a used-book store on Grande Avenue," he said.

"Not Secondhand Rows?" I asked.

"Yeah, that's the one," he said. "Have you been there?"

"Not much, but my dad really likes it," I said. "The woman who runs it is helping him find stuff for his collection of Louis L'Amour westerns. Is that your mom?"

"Always dressed in tie-dyed T-shirts and jeans?"

I laughed, nodding. "That's the one. Hey, she's nice."

Scott smiled. "Yeah, she'll do."

I was really enjoying this conversation, and I wanted to keep it going, but then I glanced at my watch. "Um, Ter, it's late," I said tentatively. Ter had to get to work. And since she was my transportation, we had to get going so she could drop me off at my house in time to make it into downtown SLO.

"Ugh," Ter said, grimacing. She smiled apologetically at Lou. "We're gainfully employed, and I guess we'd better get going if we're gonna to stay that way."

Lou glanced at his watch, looking surprised and annoyed at the same time. "Oh, yeah, so are we." He sent a look at Scott. "I have to get going or my dad'll get on my case. See you tonight?"

"Yeah." Scott nodded and fished in his pocket, pulling out a set of keys. He looked at Ter and me. "I guess we all have to get going. We'll see you tomorrow?"

From the way they were showing interest in Ter and me, maybe they didn't have flocks of girls after all, I thought. I slid a look at Teresa. She seemed to be mesmerized. "Yeah. See you

32

tomorrow," I said, nudging Ter.

I took Ter by the elbow and quickly steered her toward the parking lot. She got into the car and drove out of the parking lot without saying a word. But as soon as we got on the road, she honked her horn ten times and squealed a sound of pure joy.

"Ter!" I said in surprise. "What are you trying to do, get us arrested for disturbing the peace?" I shook my head and laughed at her. Her emotions were so infectious that I couldn't help but feel incredibly high too.

"I can't believe it!" she shouted. "Those hunks picked *us* out of the whole orchestra. Us!" Disbelief colored her every syllable. "Didn't they seem nice?" she asked, her dark eyes shining.

"Yeah," I admitted. "They did seem nice. Not at all what I would've expected."

"Why? What did you expect?" she asked, confused.

"Oh, I don't know," I said. "I guess I didn't really think about it."

"Well, I did! As soon as I saw Lou in orchestra, I just knew he was different."

"Different? How?" I asked.

Ter shrugged. "Well, I figured that if he was in orchestra, that meant he was a musician," she began. "And you know how they say artists and musicians are these tortured sensitive types?"

I tried to stifle my laughter. "Ter, did those two look like they were tortured?"

"You know what I mean!" she said impatiently. "If they're musicians, then they must have a gentle side, a tender side, a more sensitive personality. It just works that way."

"It does?" My tone was full of barely disguised mirth. Ter's a nut. That's why I love her so much. Any time I'm in danger of taking life too seriously, Ter comes along and brings out the craziness of it all.

"It does," Ter said firmly. Then she threw me a look that told me I'd better not say anything more. "And besides that," Ter continued, "he's not just a musician, he's a drummer! Lou's perfect for me. I'm done with all those muscle-bound macho types."

I bit the inside of my cheek to prevent myself from pointing out that Lou seemed to be working toward becoming a muscle-bound type. Maybe not macho, though, I reflected, remembering how embarrassed he actually seemed about admitting that he worked out.

"And another thing," Ter went on. "They're musicians and *we're* musicians. Don't you remember what we used to wish for, Krista? Can you think of a better reason for us to become couples?"

I burst out laughing and looked at Ter with affection. When we were in junior high we used to sit on the steps of Ter's house, baby-sitting her little brother, Ricardo, who's six years younger than us. While he ran around like a wild child, torturing neighborhood girls and roughhousing with the boys, Ter and I would spend hours dreaming up the criteria for our perfect boyfriends. We were like engineers, planning a dam. Our requirements had been precise and unbending. We had wanted our boyfriends to be reasonably good-looking. They also had to be intelligent and have a good sense of humor. And we really, *really* wanted them to have an interest in music, like we did. The idea of all four of us playing music together had just seemed so neat to our twelve-year-old minds. I hadn't cared what instrument my guy would play, but Ter had been more specific. "Drummers are always energetic people," she would say. "They seem so full of life. I definitely want a drummer." But our toughest demand was that our ideal boys had to be friends with each other, so we could date as a foursome. Of course, when you're twelve, you think this is something that can be easily achieved. But in reality, Ter and I learned later, boys don't necessarily like to run in coed quartets.

"No," I agreed indulgently. "No, I can't."

three

After orchestra the next day, Ter and I were chatting with Cathy as we exited the room. When we got out into the hall, we spotted her twin brother, Gavin, talking to Scott and Lou. We approached their group, and I noticed that Lou seemed to be in a particularly upbeat mood.

"Man, that is the best way to end the day," he said with a huge smile on his face. "Doing music."

Scott made a sour face. "Right. Orchestra. B-o-r-i-n-g."

"Why boring?" I asked, jumping into the discussion.

Scott turned to look at me, then grinned. "'Cause I'd rather do rock than Bach."

We all laughed, then Cathy sidled up to her brother. "Hey," she said, touching him on the shoulder. "We have to go straight home tonight, remember?"

Gavin seemed slightly irritated. "Oh, yeah, that's right," he said. "We have to take my mom up to see my grandmother," he said to the group. "So I guess I'll see you all tomorrow."

"Bye!" Cathy said with a wave.

Brother and sister left, and the four of us stood around, looking at each other awkwardly. Finally Lou spoke and tried to pick up the previous conversation from where they left off. "Well, you get your chance to do rock at my place on some nights," he said to Scott. "We can play whatever music we like then."

"You guys play drums and the cello at home?" I asked with interest.

The guys laughed, then Lou explained. "No, we play a lot of different instruments. I play the drums, keyboard, and acoustical guitar." He nodded in Scott's direction. "And he plays both electric and acoustical guitar. He just learned the cello so he could be in orchestra with me in ninth grade."

"Why did I ever listen to you?" Scott said, half in jest.

"Because I wanted someone to join me in my misery," Lou responded.

"Misery?" Ter said. "If orchestra's so bad, why did you join?"

Lou turned his warm brown eyes on Ter. "Well, it's like this. For a long time I was a self-taught musician, and joining orchestra seemed like a good way to get free lessons."

"And, man, he needed them," Scott teased.

Lou grinned at him and continued his explanation. "My folks can't afford music lessons—not with four kids in the family," he said. "Like when my sister, Magdalena, wanted to learn the piano, she had to spend her own hard-earned dollars on a portable keyboard. Then she had to learn the technique herself."

"Yeah," Scott put in, laughing. "Then Mr. Perfect came along, and she married him and lost interest in the keyboard."

"Right," Lou said. "So I got it." He laughed, then went on. "And lucky for me, my brother Raul wanted to be another Richie Valens on the guitar, until real life knocked on the door in the form of Miss Perfect. . . . And now he's a married man with kids."

"Let me guess," I said, smiling. "You got a guitar out of it."

"You got it," he said.

"And the drums?" Ter prompted.

Lou was silent, and a shadow crossed over his face. I glanced over at Scott. He looked uncomfortable too. After a while, Lou said simply, "My other brother, Roberto, left them behind when he . . . moved out."

I immediately sensed a tightness in his voice and I made a mental note not to bring up the subjects of drums or his brother ever again. Ter had a puzzled look on her face, but she didn't say anything.

"So, do you two play anything but violins?" Lou asked, suddenly very upbeat.

"You bet we do," Ter answered proudly. "I play the piano, and Krista plays acoustical guitar. And sometimes we have jam sessions together at her house or mine."

Scott brightened. "Hey, you know what?" he said excitedly. "With all these instruments, we could play together. We could form a band of our own."

"Yeah," Lou agreed. He looked at Teresa, smiling broadly. "We could switch off on the keyboard," he suggested to her.

"Or play a duet," Scott suggested.

"Yeah!" Ter exclaimed. She smiled at Lou, trying not to look too eager. If I hadn't been her best friend, I wouldn't have known how she was feeling. But I was, and I did know. She was fit to be held down by ropes to keep her from floating off.

The guys began walking toward the senior

lockers, and without really thinking about it, Ter and I followed. The layout of our school is typical of California: all the classroom doors lead directly outside, and most of the lockers are spread out along the open-air walkways. The *senior* lockers, however, are located indoors, in one of the school's nicer wings. One of the special privileges of being a senior, I guess.

So we were headed toward the senior lockers, with Scott talking very seriously about the four of us forming a band. He wanted us all to get together sometime soon, so that we could hear each other play and determine whether we sounded good enough to get gigs. The more he talked, the better it sounded.

After a couple of minutes, Lou and Ter dropped back to walk together behind me and Scott. I glanced over my shoulder and thought they looked so good together. I hoped this would work out for Ter. I really wanted someone to like her the way she deserved to be liked. And Lou somehow seemed like the perfect guy for her. I had sat with Ter through a lot of crying sessions—even on the phone, long-distance, when I lived in Seattle—and I knew how vulnerable she was. Though she always recovered from her ordeals and heartaches quickly, the pain she had inside never really went away. I didn't want Lou to cause her more pain.

"So what do you think?" Scott asked as I paused next to my locker.

"Well . . ." I began.

"Hey, how did you get one on the top?" he said, referring to my locker. "I thought the people in the office never gave tall people the high lockers."

Our lockers were tiny, practically useless compartments, stacked three high. I giggled. "I see you've noticed the same thing I have. Sometimes I think the person who assigns lockers looks at each student's statistics, then chooses the worst possible locker position. So we end up with low ones for tall people—"

"And high ones for short people," Scott said, laughing.

"Right," I said. "So when Ter got her original locker assignment, she had one on the top row. And I had one on the lowest row. So we simply switched—I learned her combination, she learned mine, and now we're both happy."

Scott looked at Lou and smiled. "Amigo, I'd like to make a deal with you."

"Don't tell me," Lou said, pretending to be wary. "You want my combination."

"You guys have the same problem we did?" Ter asked.

"Yep. But soon we'll have that problem solved, right, amigo?" Scott joked.

Lou smiled and shook his head slowly. "No chance, buddy," he said. "I may not be as tall as you, but I'm not *that* short."

We all laughed, then Scott shrugged and turned back to me. "So, when do you think we can all get together and play some music?" he asked.

He was obviously serious about forming a band, and I didn't quite know what to say. I mean, the four of us had met only the day before. "I'll have to think about it," I said, looking up at him. "You know . . . look at my work schedule and all."

"Good enough," he said affably. He punched Lou on the arm. "Hey, amigo. We'd better hit the road if we're going to make it to SLO on time."

"Oh, yeah," Lou said, his eyes still on Ter. He had been talking to her about something, and he'd seemed to be giving her his total attention.

"We'll catch you guys tomorrow," Scott said, smiling at me.

"Mañana," Lou said with a wave.

I turned to Ter. She looked as if she were going to burst out of her skin. I could tell she was trying to keep herself in check until the guys were out of sight; she had her mouth clamped shut to keep back the laughter. We couldn't get off campus fast enough. We grabbed our stuff from our lockers, then raced to her car.

As soon as we dropped into the front seats, Ter screamed. "Oh, I cannot believe it!" Then, once she had calmed down a bit, she asked, "Am I crazy, or does it look like Lou likes me?"

"You're not crazy," I assured her. "It *does* look like he likes you. And you guys make a great-looking couple."

"So do you and Scott," she said. "You're both blond and tall and gorgeous."

"Stop, Ter! My head's swelling," I said, pretending to hold my skull in. "But seriously, Ter," I added earnestly. "I hope this is the one." I put my hand on her shoulder. "I hope Lou's the guy I told you was going to come along some day."

"Oh, I hope he is too," Ter said fervently. For a minute, she just sat there, staring dreamily out the windshield. "He really seems special," she said. "I can feel it. You know, when I talk to him, he looks like he's really listening. Not like that creep Carlos—Carlos just wanted me to be quiet and decorative." Ter started the car, put it in gear, then gave me a mischievous look. "You know, the four of us really could form a band—you and Scott, me and Lou. We'd be two couples making great music." She laughed delightedly, throwing her head back. "Krista, can't you just see it?"

"Maybe," I said, not feeling quite as enthusiastic as Ter. It *was* a great idea to form a band, but Ter was already making Scott and me into a couple, and I really wasn't sure that was what I wanted.

My mother is trying to train me to be a good cook. One night a week she teaches me how to prepare all kinds of food. When I got home that evening, Mom announced that it was time for another cooking lesson.

"Okay, Mom," I said. "I'll be down in two minutes."

I ran up to my room to change, and when I came down to the kitchen, my mother was busy studying a cookbook on the counter in front of her. She had it propped up in one of those Lucite cookbook holders, the kind that keeps the opened book behind plastic so you won't spill on the pages. I don't know why she even bothered. She never spills anything. Anyway, she'd decided that we would cook French that night—homemade French onion soup.

Before long, Mom was patiently showing me the correct way of putting the cheese on fat slices of French bread. I was looking at her, but my eyes weren't seeing anything. Instead, I kept picturing two guys and Ter and me playing in a band. Ever since Scott had come up with the idea after school, it was all I could think about. Could we really become a band? Would we be good enough to actually get paid to play at dances and things? Ter and I had our own personal jam sessions sometimes, but so far only our families had heard us play. They hadn't covered their ears when they heard us, so I figured we probably weren't all that bad. But were we *good*? I wondered.

"You're awfully spacey tonight," my mother said, sounding annoyed. "Here, let me have the measuring cup."

I relinquished the glass cup to her. "Mom, I don't see why we have to measure every time. Why can't we just estimate how much a quarter cup of grated cheese is?"

"*I* could," she said. "But you can't. You need to measure many, many times before you can begin estimating things. That's the point of this whole exercise." Her tone implied that she had told me this a thousand times, and she had.

"Okay," I said, watching her measure out the first portion of cheese and place it very precisely on a piece of bread floating in onion soup. I looked around the kitchen, which had all the culinary touches she'd demanded: granite counter tops, a six-burner stainless-steel stove, and a center island with a built-in coupling for her food processor and blender. In one corner of the kitchen stood an appliance garage containing a toaster, a crock pot, and a can opener. I wasn't sure I liked such absolute precision and order. I lean more toward a cluttered existence, which is probably why my mother had suddenly decided to teach me how to use the kitchen. Maybe she hoped to override my natural tendency to be a little bit messy by teaching me only the neat, organized way to do everything.

"When do we get the grub?" Dad asked, ambling into the room.

"Eric! It's not *grub*," my mother said irritably. "Do you have to call it that?"

I beamed at him from behind my mother's back. Mom and I are alike only in looks. In all other respects, I take after my father. And to me, it was grub, too.

"Okay, Susan," my father said with a huge grin. "When do we get the repast?"

"In ten minutes," she said, trying not to laugh.

"Great!" he said, ambling back out.

Normally I don't mind my mother's cooking lessons, but that night I really wasn't up to it. I wished I could just grab a bowl of cold cereal and eat it up in my room, like I do when my mother works late at the bank, where she's the executive loan officer. I wanted to mull over the band idea and talk to Ter about it on the phone.

When my mother and I had finally finished up

in the kitchen, the three of us sat down to eat at the Queen Anne dining table in our formal dining room. I prefer to eat in the breakfast nook in the kitchen, but my mother insists we sit in the dining room at dinnertime. My father and I tried not to slurp the soup.

"You've outdone yourselves again," my father said with approval. "Good grub," he added with a wink at me.

My mother sighed in exasperation, and I tried to suppress a giggle.

The meal lasted forever. But finally, after helping clean up, I raced up to my room. I had Ter's number dialed on my phone before I even fell on the bed. We talked for almost an hour about the pros and cons of forming a band with Scott and Lou. One major problem was how we were going to work it into our school and work schedules. We had to practice violin at least every other day, and we both worked three nights a week. Plus, we would have to coordinate our schedules with theirs.

"We're probably jumping the gun, anyway," I said. "I mean, we haven't even agreed to meet and hear each other play yet."

"Well, I say we talk to the guys tomorrow," Ter resolved. "We'll talk to them after orchestra and get everything straight. Okay?"

"Okay," I agreed.

Ter approached Lou right after orchestra the next day. "Lou," she said, timidly placing her hand on his arm.

He turned around and smiled when he saw her, and I noticed that his eyes crinkled at the corners too, like Scott's. "Hi. How's it going?" he asked. But I could tell he was just being polite. Clearly, something else was on his mind.

"Um, great," Ter said, unsure of herself. Her eyes were darting back and forth as if she were struggling with what she was going to say next.

"Good practice today, huh?" Lou said awkwardly.

"Yeah, great," Ter agreed, nodding.

"Pretty soon we'll sound like we're all reading the same sheet of music," he said.

I laughed, and some of the tension seemed to dissipate. "You sound like Dan Nguyen," I said.

Lou put on a horrified expression. "Oh no, do you think it's terminal?"

Ter giggled despite her discomfort. "Don't worry," she said. "You're safe. We're the ones who sit next to him. You sit too far away to catch anything from him."

"Whew," Lou said, wiping his brow.

"Hey, where's Scott today?" I asked. "Is he sick or something?"

"No, he had to go meet with his guidance counselor. Something about college applications," Lou said, smiling at me. Then he glanced at his watch and grimaced. "Look, uh, I have to run," he said apologetically. "I have to, uh, go visit someone."

Ter looked at her own watch. "Yeah. We have to get going too," she said. "Work."

"Where exactly do you two work?" he asked, suddenly sounding interested in what we were saying.

"Well, I work at a flower shop in San Luis," Ter replied. "And Krista works at the Taco Bell on Santa Rosa."

Lou nodded. "You girls have a hefty commute."

"Yeah, but at least we have jobs," I said.

"True," Lou said, nodding. He smiled and looked at Ter. "I'd better go. See you." He turned and strode out the door.

Tongue-tied, Ter watched him go. The expression on her face resembled that of a diabetic gazing at a forbidden dessert. When he was out of sight, she said, "Well, so much for the band idea."

I didn't saying anything, because I really didn't know what I could say to make her feel better. I simply shrugged and started off toward our lockers.

Ter sighed heavily. Twice. Then she said in a forlorn voice, "Oh, well. He was probably just like all the others. I'm probably lucky to have been spared from another heavy romance. Singlehood is so much less confining. And spinsterhood is sounding better and better all the—"

"Come on, Ter," I said, amazed that she could still kid around when I knew her heart was cracking. "It's obvious he had something on his mind. And it's Scott's idea about the band, anyway. If he had been here, he probably would have brought it up again. So we'll just have to wait and see what happens next, okay?"

"I hate waiting to see what happens next," Ter said vehemently.

four

The following night I had to work at Taco Bell. It was a pretty slow night, and by around eight thirty, things really began to die down. All the people who wanted dinner had come and gone, and the late-night snackers hadn't arrived yet. I was keeping busy trying to make Ernesto think I was busy. I polished all the stainless-steel surfaces, neatened the stacks of paper cups, and even checked that all the napkin dispensers were full. I was going mad. I hate the slow times. The minutes crawl, and you're too conscious of how long you have to wait until quitting time. And since I'd borrowed my mother's car that night, I couldn't even look forward to Ter dropping in early to take me home.

Finally, when I was seriously thinking about hunting down Ernesto and actually asking for work, the door opened, and two customers came in. I quickly made my way over to the front counter to take their orders, and suddenly realized that the two guys approaching were Scott and Lou!

"Hi," Scott said, grinning widely. He leaned his elbow against the counter. "Someone happened to mention that you work here, and we just happened to be driving by and—"

"Oh, yeah?" I said, amused. Scott laughed and over his shoulder, I saw Lou trying to hide a smile. Right. They just happened to be twenty some miles out of their way, up in San Luis. It was possible, I supposed. But I doubted it.

"So when do you get off work?" Scott asked.

"Ten."

"Ten, huh?" He looked at his watch. "An hour and a half away."

"A *long* hour and a half," I said, sighing.

The door swung open again, and the first batch of late-night snackers came in, a gang of about seven guys. I recognized Carlos in the group. *Oh great,* I thought, *now I can get back at him by sprinkling enormous quantities of extra hot pepper on his food.* I can get pretty hostile with guys who treat Ter shabbily. But Suzanne, the other attendant on duty, had already spotted him and rushed up to take his order, oozing interest.

I turned back to Scott, trying not to show my disgust. "Did you want anything?" I asked.

"Yeah," he said, cocking his head to one side. "But you don't get off for an hour and a half."

I felt a blush beginning to creep up into my face, and I laughed lightly.

"Hey, how about if you and Teresa come out with Lou and me tomorrow night?" he asked. "Do you have to work?" He raised his eyebrows in a hopeful expression.

"Umm, I'll have to check with Ter," I answered.

"Great. What's your phone number?" he asked, biting his lower lip. "I'll call in the morning and find out what you two decided."

I gave it to him, then caught sight of Ernesto glaring at me from his office door. The man is paranoid about his employees loafing. Hastily I snagged a burrito from behind me and shoved it at Scott. "Here's your order," I said brightly. Ernesto came over and hovered within two feet of me like a demented hummingbird, and I shifted on my feet nervously. To my relief Scott had the presence of mind to take the burrito and pay for it. Then, he gave me a wink and sauntered out of the restaurant. Lou followed right behind him.

True to his word, Scott called the next morning.

I had spoken to Ter as soon as I got home the night before, and of course she'd agreed to go out with the guys. The invitation had certainly come as I surprise to her, though. After how Lou had acted at orchestra, Ter wasn't feeling particularly hopeful about dating him.

After I had told Scott that it was okay with Ter, I was expecting him to get off the phone right away. But instead he started chatting away about everything: our jobs, music, school, how we thought we'd do on the SATs . . .

"My parents are super serious about me scoring in the top percentiles," he lamented. "They want me to go to a good college. I don't know why they're so obsessed. I mean, they already have one child at a good school."

"Oh yeah?" I said, staring up at my ceiling. I was lying on my back, using the flat white painted surface as a sort of movie screen. Scott's face, conjured up from my memory, was playing on it. As he spoke, I tried to imagine what his expression was like.

"Yeah. My older sister Karen's at Vassar in New York State," he said. "And all *I* want to do is be a musician." His words made me paint a yearning expression on his face. "What do I need math and science for?"

I understood how he felt, even though I didn't share his feelings. "But think of it this way," I suggested. "When you start earning all your millions, you'll need math to know if your accountant is honest."

Scott groaned. "You sound just like Lou," he said. "And like I told him, I'd hire Karen. She's the big math star in the family. And she'd never gyp her baby brother." Now I imagined a smile playing across his face.

"Okay, I'm convinced," I said. "Run down to your guidance counselor on Monday and tell him you're cutting some of your classes out. Say you're a conscientious objector, refusing to take any course that won't further your musical career."

Scott laughed heartily, conveying his genuine appreciation for the joke. "That would eliminate everything except orchestra," he said. The tone of his voice made me picture a grin on his face. "But I still say I'd rather do rock than Bach."

I laughed. "Just remember, lots of big stars had classical training, like Elton John and—"

"Wow, now you really do sound like Lou," Scott said, half in disgust and half in disbelief.

"He tells you that too?" I asked, surprised for some reason.

"Yeah, he does all the time," he said.

We finally hung up about an hour after he called, with Scott saying he and Lou would pick us up at five.

By four fifty-three that afternoon, Ter's and my nerves were shot. She had come over to my house at four to wait, and we'd killed time sitting in the living room trying to convince each other that we were not candidates for straight jackets; waiting for two gorgeous guys to pick us up on a double date was something we experienced so often it verged on boredom.

We had both chosen our outfits carefully. Ter was wearing a pair of black leggings and a brightly printed trapeze top. I was wearing white stirrup pants and a top Ter had given me. She's forever buying stuff, then hating the way she looks in them. So she always ends up giving clothes to me, and I'll say, "But you look adorable in this." Her rebuttal is always the same: "Give me a break. I look like a mushroom cloud in that." "But mushrooms don't come in Forenza multi-colored stripes," I'll argue. Then she'll bat at the air, saying, "I'm talking about the general shape." I usually give up and take the clothes. Once Ter's mind is made up, dynamite can't move her. So anyway, I had on one of her rejects. A Forenza crop top in beautiful earth tones, accented with turquoise, which Ter claims makes my eyes look bluer.

Ter was sitting on the sofa, pleating and repleating the edges of her trapeze top. As expected, her nerves went before mine. "Oh, I can't take it anymore," she said, bounding to her feet to peer through the gauzy drapes at the front window. She was careful to keep out of sight in case the guys arrived and caught her in the act. "Krista, I really have this feeling down here—" She pointed to the region of her stomach. "—that this is it!"

"That's your stomach, Ter," I said drily. "You have indigestion."

"Oh, you know what I mean!" She narrowed her dark brown eyes at me, but she was giggling.

I laughed, watching her try to get as close to the drapes as possible without actually touching them. "So why do you think this is it?"

She turned back, her eyes sparkling like two pieces of polished glass. "Because Lou is so different, so nice! And he's a drummer, just like I wanted," she said dreamily. "Krista, you couldn't take a computer program and have it design a more perfect guy." She frowned suddenly. "Which is why I can't understand why he'd be interested in me, but that's beside the point." She waved her hand at the irritating thought.

"You want a refresher course in how wonderful you are?" I asked, half teasing. "I'll tell you. Because you're adorable and fun loving. You're bubbly. . . ." I paused, searching for the right words.

Ter grinned unabashedly. "More, more," she said, bursting into laughter. "My head's not the right size yet."

"Ter, I'm serious. Why would anyone not like you?" I said.

She opened her mouth, then seemed to think better of what she'd been about to say. "Scott really seems to like you, too," she said instead. She tipped her head to one side. "Aren't you just a little bit thrilled?"

"Well, I'll wait and see," I said, taking the cautious approach. "I don't even really know him yet. And remember, you don't really know Lou either."

Ter shook her head and shrugged. "But what more could there be to know?" she said, looking at me.

Oh, Ter, I thought. You're so impulsive. And too trusting. But then again, maybe I had gone through so many of Ter's romantic disasters that I could no longer recognize a great guy for her when I saw one. But what if this guy, this "perfect" guy, hurt her? What if he cheated on her or dumped her for someone else? It would break her heart worse than ever before. I *had* to look out for Ter.

The doorbell suddenly rang, startling us both. "They're here!" Ter all but screamed. She quickly clamped her hand over her mouth. "Oh, do you think they heard that?"

"I doubt it," I said reassuringly. "My father built this house like a fortress." I headed for the door, and Ter raced behind me and peeked out the side window.

"It is them," she affirmed. Then, turning to me with a smug look on her face, she said, "See? They *are* perfect. They came to the door instead of honking. Your parents will appreciate that."

I opened the door, unable to stop a giddy smile from forming on my face. Scott and Lou looked a little uneasy at first, but they returned my smile when I pulled the door open wider.

"Come on in," I said. They hesitated a little, and I explained in a voice of someone confessing a horrible sin, "My parents insist on meeting you."

"Ah," Scott said, nodding his head knowingly. He stepped into the house with Lou right on his heels.

My parents came into the room before I even had a chance to call them, no doubt having heard the commotion, and I made the introductions as swiftly as possible. I hate it when my parents subject any boy crazy enough to want to date me to the third degree. "It is not the third degree," they insist, but it is. This time, however, my parents couldn't figure out which of the two guys was my date, so they let us go without much of an interview. And soon the four of us were backing out of the house and making our escape.

"What time will you be home?" my parents chorused as we were closing the front door.

"Oh, after dark," I said, leaving a lot of leeway.

We pounded down the drive and leaped into Scott's Jeep. Laughing and wiping our brows in mock relief, we took off.

"So, where do you guys want to go?" Scott asked, rounding the corner onto Grande Avenue.

"Well, I'm starved," Lou announced.

"So tell me something I don't know," Scott teased, grinning at his friend in the rearview mirror. "Amigo, it's only five o'clock. It's too early for food."

"That's what I get for hanging around with a guy whose parents never eat," Lou joked.

Scott smiled and glanced over at me. "My mom hates to cook," he explained. "She says she'd rather 'read than feed.' She spends a lot of time at her bookstore, and when she's not there, she's with my dad at the surf shop."

I thought of my own mother and her cooking fetish. "So what do you do for meals?" I asked.

Scott nodded in the direction of the backseat. "Lou feeds me."

"Oh," I said. I looked into the back and noticed that Lou had his arm stretched out along the top of the seat behind Ter. Ter must be in heaven, I thought to myself, feeling thrilled for her.

As we drove on, we continued to discuss what we were going to do for the evening. But Lou couldn't seem to think of anything but food.

"Stop whining," Scott said to him. "We have to do something interesting first. That way, when we actually get to the eating establishment of our choice, you'll enjoy the feeding process that much more."

"Yeah, right," Lou said dubiously. Then he brightened. "Hey, we could go to the movies," he suggested. "That way I can stave off impending starvation with junk food."

We agreed on Lou's plan and headed for the fourplex theater, where we bought tickets to the latest Nerds movie. Before long, the four of us were sitting in darkness, passing around a huge bucket of buttered popcorn and laughing hysterically. I heard Lou whisper to Ter that it was going to be difficult to feed a body whose intestines were bruised by all the laughing, but that didn't prove to be a problem later on. After the movie, we went to a pizza place and tried to order a pie that would please everyone.

"We want a designer pizza," Scott told the waitress with a smile.

"What do you want on it?" she asked.

Scott hunched his shoulders forward, as if concentrating on a very difficult problem. "We want one quarter of it to be sausage with mushrooms and onions—"

"And one quarter to be pepperoni and green peppers," Ter added, getting into the spirit of things.

"Have you got any jalapeno peppers?" Lou asked hopefully.

The girl stared at him dumbly.

"Amigo, if you want jalapenos, you'd better go home," Scott said with a straight face. "This is an *Italian* restaurant."

Lou feigned surprise. "It is? Whose idea was it to come here?"

Everyone laughed, but the waitress looked a little irritated. So we took pity on her and finished up our order.

While we waited for the pizza, Scott brought up the idea of us playing for each other again.

"So have you girls thought about it?" he asked.

"Yeah," I said, glancing at Ter. "We'd like to give it a try."

"Great! Let's get together tomorrow at Lou's," Scott said enthusiastically. "That's where we usually practice. We can set up your instruments and see how we sound."

I don't know if it was just an impulsive move or

not, but right then Scott reached out and took my hand. He held it for a while as we talked. To say I was surprised would be an understatement. So far Lou had made no physical moves on Ter, which certainly broke the pattern of the kind of guys she usually dated. And I was a little uncomfortable with Scott showing this kind of affection publicly.

After we had had our pizza, we left the restaurant, discussing what time we'd get together the next day. Since we didn't know where Lou lived and we weren't familiar with the address, Scott offered to pick us up. I tried to imagine the four of us as a band, playing for money . . . dressed up in costumes . . . but the image wouldn't gel. Trying to picture it was like watching figures through frosted glass. Maybe that was because we hadn't actually played yet, and I needed more details to really flesh out the fantasy.

Scott took us to my house, since that's where Ter's car was parked. We broke off in pairs, trying to give each other some space and privacy. It was difficult, though. My rotten parents had turned on the driveway spotlights and the two coach lights flanking the front door. It was as bright as daylight outside my house. A definite hindrance to romance.

Scott steered me over to a shadow cast by a

birch tree at the side of the driveway. "I really enjoyed tonight," he said, taking me into his arms. Then he kissed me on the lips good night, and I kissed him back, not knowing how to stop him. I didn't really want to kiss him; but then, I didn't *not* want to kiss him either. And besides, I didn't see the harm in a simple kiss.

Finally, Scott walked me to the door, and Lou and Ter came up behind us. We all sort looked around, smiling awkwardly before saying our final good-byes and thank yous. Then, after the guys had driven away, Ter and I went into my house and closed the door.

"A-h-h-h!" Ter said, whispering so as not to disturb my parents. "I can't wait till tomorrow."

five

When Scott came to get us the next day, Ter climbed into the backseat of his Jeep with my guitar. She was going to use Lou's electric keyboard, so she didn't have to bring any instruments with her. As we drove into Lou's neighborhood, I looked around with interest. He lived on a little cul-de-sac on the edge of a village, where they didn't even have curbs and sidewalks. The street was dusty, and most of the yards were small and bare. I knew he didn't come from particularly wealthy parents. That's why he was in orchestra, instead of studying music privately. But I wasn't expecting quite such a depressing neighborhood.

Lou's house was one of those early California

types with peach-colored wood siding and a high pitched hip roof. There was a garage built separately from the house, and the front yard looked manicured and lush with well-tended grass, bordered by colorful flowerbeds. Deep red bougainvillea bushes grew above a stockade fence between his house and the next, and a neat row of sunflowers, their heads drooping over sideways, stood behind a massive bed of smaller flowers.

We unloaded our instruments—Scott's two guitars, a six string and a four string, and my own—and hauled them into the garage. An amplifier for Scott's guitar was already set up in the garage, and I could see how really serious he was about his music. Lou had his set of drums in one corner, and I noticed a set of weights and a bench in another. I raised an eyebrow at Ter and nodded toward the weights. She looked at them and grinned.

"Let's go see what Lou's up to in the house," Scott said. He led us out of the garage and across a small patio. Pungent smells wafted through the screened back door of the house. Without knocking, Scott pushed the door open and walked in. Ter and I followed hesitantly.

Lou was standing by the stove, stirring something in a huge kettle. "You're just in time to get out the chips and dump 'em in a bowl," he said to Scott. He winked at Ter and smiled at me.

Scott went directly to a cabinet and took out a bowl. Obviously he was used to moving around in the Pacheco kitchen.

"I've got salsa in the fridge all made up. Get that out," Lou said over his shoulder as he continued to stir whatever it was he was cooking.

"Great!" Scott said. "Have you got chili con queso too?"

Lou grinned at him. "Scott, when have I ever failed to have your favorite snack?" He nodded at a small pot on the back burner. "Dump it in something, will you?"

Scott moved over next to him and reached into a cabinet above Lou's head. He brought down a small ceramic dish.

"And while you're up there," Lou said, "get me the pisilla chili and the cumin, will you?"

"What's cumin?" Scott asked, reaching into the cabinet again.

"Good eats is comin', man, good eats," Lou said with a laugh. Then he reached up and snagged two spice jars out of the cabinet. "If you want to eat my food," he said to Scott, "you've got to learn how to identify the ingredients."

"Naw, I'll just confuse myself if I know too much," Scott said, grinning over at Ter and me. We were standing just inside the back door. Ter looked stupefied. I don't think she'd ever seen a male do anything that smacked of work in the kitchen.

Ter and I sidled up to the stove to see what Lou had in the pot. He stirred the red mass and then tasted it. "Not enough salt," he announced, shaking his head. He reached for a salt container, poured some into the palm of his hand, and dropped it into the pot.

"You wash that hand?" Scott teased.

"Yeah, in the dog's water dish, like always," Lou replied, punching Scott in the shoulder. He placed a lid on the pot.

"You have a dog?" Ter asked, looking around the room.

Lou grinned and nodded toward the screened door. "Yeah, he's out there somewhere in the yard."

"Really?" I said. "But he didn't bark when we came in."

"A Pacheco dog never barks," Scott said in a serious tone.

Lou shook his head, chuckling. "That's right," he said. "My mother always said that with four kids, there was enough noise. So any dog we ever had was taught that barking is a no-no." He and Scott smiled and exchanged meaningful looks. The silence that followed seemed to be touched with a trace of sorrow. Ter looked as if she also sensed the sudden change in the mood, and her eyes were darting around the room.

Lou looked at us with his dark eyes, the smile wrinkles at the corners deepening. "You girls ready to play?"

"You bet," Ter said, already stepping backward toward the screened door.

I nodded in agreement. But I was ready to vacate the aromatic kitchen for a different reason. The room smelled of chili powder, cumin, and all those other mysterious spices associated with Mexican food, and I was reminded of my work at Taco Bell. Anything that reminded me of work was not welcome, and I wanted to escape to the garage as swiftly as possible.

Lou raised his arms and began herding us out of the kitchen. "Okay, let's go," he said, backing us out through the door. But just then a woman dressed in a nursing uniform entered the kitchen. As soon as I saw her, I knew she had to be his mother. He looked so much like her.

She spotted the large pot on the stove, walked straight over to it, and lifted off the lid. "Oh, no!" she exclaimed in mock horror. "Not another batch of your killer chili." She replaced the lid and looked at her son with a woebegone expression. "What bad thing did I do as a child, that I ended up with a son who's always cooking?"

Lou grinned. "I have to cook," he said to her. "It's the only way I ever get enough to eat around here. With you and dad working crazy shifts all the time, I have no choice but to do it myself."

"Oh, you poor, poor undernourished boy," his mother said sarcastically. Then she turned to the rest of us and smiled. "So this is the band, eh?" she said, addressing Lou.

"Ter, Krista," Lou said. "This is my mother."

We both said hello politely, and his mother smiled warmly at us. Then she suddenly scowled at Lou and lifted an admonishing finger. "And afterwards, clean up this mess!" she said sternly, but there was a smile tugging at the corners of her mouth.

Lou sent her an innocent look. "Don't I always?" he asked.

"Sure, sure," his mother said as she started toward the hallway leading from the kitchen. "After everything's sat in the sink for three days and you need a blow torch for the job."

Scott laughed. "She knows you too well, amigo."

Lou just smiled and went over to check his killer chili one more time. I really wasn't sure I wanted to sample something with such an ominous name. The smells pouring out of the pot were overpowering. "So you cook a lot, huh?" I asked.

"*Does* he?" Scott said, making a sound that can only be described as a cross between a snort and a hoot. "If he wasn't going to be a famous musician, he'd be a famous chef!"

Mrs. Pacheco came back into the kitchen then and glanced over at her son stirring his creation. She shook her head and said, "Some girl's going to love you because she'll never have to cook."

"Uh-uh," Lou said, shaking his head from side to side. "I'm going to find one who loves to cook too, and we'll cook side by side."

His mother laughed and slung a brown shoulder bag over her arm. "Then you'll both be *gordo*!" she said.

"Yeah, but we'll have lots to love!"

We all laughed, and Mrs. Pacheco headed toward the screen door. Ter and I stepped out of her way. "I'm off to work," she said. "Have fun, kids, and don't drive the neighbors to commit murder with your music."

The door slammed behind her and a few seconds later I heard a car start up and back out of the driveway.

"What a woman you've got for a mother," Scott said, teasing Lou.

"She just doesn't appreciate me like she should. She should be glad I cook," Lou said, pretending to complain.

71

"My mother makes me do a lot of cooking," I blurted out suddenly.

"Oh really?" Lou asked, looking at me with interest.

"Yeah. It's a requirement that any child of hers must know her way around the kitchen," I explained. "The thing is, it's deadly serious business to her. We *never*, ever measure anything in the palm of our hand," I said with mock severity.

"You actually use those funny little spoons that all fit together?" Lou asked, joining in the joke.

"Yup. And we use measuring cups too," I said.

"Ugh," Lou said, making a face. "My motto is: Any ingredient that requires measurement is an ingredient I can do without."

"But that must make your cooking very confining," I said.

"Naw. But it does make it inconsistent," Lou said, laughing.

Scott grabbed the bowl he'd filled with chips and handed a container of red sauce to Ter. "Hey, come on. Let's get going," he said.

"Yeah, enough about food," Ter agreed.

"Right," Lou said, reaching for the small pot on the stove. "I can't wait to hear how we sound."

We trooped out to the garage with the food, then began setting up our instruments. Scott and I set up music stands, and he plugged his electric guitar into the amplifier. Lou showed Ter the electric keyboard, and I watched as they ran through some chords together. What a great-looking couple they'd make, I thought for about the zillionth time.

After we had set everything up, we started to discuss what we'd play. It turned out that we all loved fast music and a few slower ballads. We all liked Elton John, George Michael, Heart, Prince, and countless others. The hard part wasn't agreeing on what to play; it was agreeing on what to play first.

"I think we should play an instrumental first," I suggested. "That way we can concentrate on how our instruments sound, without the distraction of trying to get our voices to mesh."

"That makes sense," Scott agreed. "Let's do it."

I was impressed. That Scott was willing to take a suggestion from me was really great. After all, it was his idea to form the band, and he could have felt that that gave him the right to make all the decisions. But he was easygoing, laid back, willing to listen to suggestions. The more I got to know Scott, the more I liked him, but I still wasn't ready to throw myself into a relationship with him.

We decided that Scott would play lead guitar on his six string, I'd play his bass, Ter would get on the keyboard, and Lou would play his drums.

"Okay," Ter said, running her fingers up and down the keyboard. "I'm all set. Why don't we just pick a song we already know just to see how we sound?"

Lou nodded. "Yeah, that's perfect."

A couple of minutes later, we had settled on an Allman Brothers' piece called *Jessica's Song*. Lou tapped out the count on his drums, and the three of us jumped in. In all honesty I can't say we sounded spectacular. In fact, I was beginning to think Mrs. Pacheco's warning about making the neighbors want to commit murder wasn't so farfetched after all.

We did several takes, and finally after about our fifth attempt, we were beginning to sound pretty good.

"I think Scott and Krista should try singing together now," Ter said brightly after we had finished another take.

Scott and I looked at each other, and then he grinned at me. "Yeah, a duet," he said a bit shyly.

I smiled back at him and nodded. "Okay," I said, trying not to seem nervous.

We ended up singing *Hold On My Heart*. Scott took the lead, and I did second voice. He was halfway between a bass and a baritone, and I'm an alto. Even to my ears, it seemed that Scott's voice and mine blended beautifully.

We finished the song, all four of us laughing.

"That's it," Scott said resolutely. "We have to form a band. We're good together. You guys agree?"

I nodded.

"And aren't they perfect singing together?" Ter asked with a nod at Scott and me.

"Yeah. We all complement each other perfectly," Lou said, smiling back at her.

Ter beamed, and I knew she was ready to go airborne.

Then Scott got up and pretended to stagger over to the food. "After that session, I really need to fortify myself," he said, stabbing a chip into one of the ceramic dishes. He popped the chip into his mouth, then turned to Lou. "Amigo, I think the salsa needs to be nuked," he said. "Our music may be hot, but this isn't."

Lou laughed, then went over to pick up the ceramic dish. He walked over to a corner of the garage where there was a long workbench. I hadn't looked closely at that part of the garage, so I hadn't noticed the small microwave oven sitting on the table. Boy, these guys are *really* serious about their food, I thought to myself.

Ter followed Lou over to the workbench and talked to him while the microwave whirred.

I was chatting with Scott and munching on some chips.

"You know, I've always wanted to form a

band," he was telling me in a low voice. "I was just waiting for the right people to come along."

I nodded, feeling vaguely flattered by what he was saying.

"It's incredible that you and Ter came along when you did," he said. "And it's even more amazing that you two seem so right for us in other ways, too." He was standing very close to me, looking down into my eyes.

I wasn't quite sure how to react to that, so I just kept on munching on the chips and smiling.

Then Lou brought the warmed salsa over to us, and we attacked the food as though we hadn't eaten in days. After the dip was polished off, we went into Lou's house and he fed us the killer chili.

"Hmmm. This is great, Lou," Ter said.

"Yeah . . . so much better than the stuff we serve at Taco Bell," I added. I was so hungry that the powerful smells of spices didn't bother me anymore.

While we were eating, Lou's dog showed up at the back door. He was a funny-looking mix of shepherd and collie, with one ear that stood up and one ear that flopped forward. Lou went over and patted him affectionately as he let him into the kitchen. Then he tossed a cube of beef from his chili into the air, and the dog snapped it up.

I held up a spoonful of the chili and looked at

Lou. "You know, this is really good," I told him sincerely. "I'll bet my boss Ernesto would pay big bucks for your recipe."

Ter feigned shock. "Ernesto! Parting with real dollars?" she exclaimed. "No way."

"You're right," I admitted. "What am I saying? Ernesto would just steal the recipe."

Everyone laughed, then we all went over to the stove for seconds. Ter and Lou reached for the ladle at the same time, so they ended up fighting for it playfully. Ter slapped Lou's arm, snatching the ladle right out of his hand. But Lou managed to take it back again by tickling her around the waist. Then finally Ter picked up a nearby cooking fork and threatened to stab him with it, so Lou raised his hands in surrender, dropping the ladle into the cooking pot. Ter giggled as she ladled out a bowlful of chili for herself, then one for Lou.

"Okay. So you won," Lou said to her good-naturedly. "There's no need to gloat."

As I watched the two of them banter back and forth, I decided that Lou qualified as the nicest guy Ter had ever dated. Though they weren't exactly *dating* yet, it certainly appeared as if they were heading in that direction. And I really hoped things would work out for Ter. Lou was funny and he seemed to look out for everyone around him. And besides, Lou cooked! That was so neat. It would be so much fun to have a guy cook for you all the time. I was amazed Lou didn't have a girlfriend. But then I had a horrifying thought. What if he did? What if there was someone else in his life, and he hadn't told Ter about her? I knew that I was entertaining ridiculous thoughts. I mean, Lou hadn't done anything to arouse suspicion. But I couldn't help it. Watching Lou talk to Ter, and watching Ter bask in his attention, was enough to make me nervous. What if, after all these years of waiting for the guy of her dreams, he came along and broke her heart?

six

After Scott took us to my house, Ter and I sat on the stoop outside and talked for a while.

"You don't think Lou is just stringing me along, do you?" she asked, her face creased in worry. She was chewing on her lip—a sure sign that she was having a case of self doubt.

"Why do you say that?" I asked.

"Because sometimes I get the feeling he's not as interested in me as I am in him," she explained. "You know. It's just a feeling." She paused for a moment. "Like, he smiles at me sometimes, but the smile isn't a whole-face one. You know what I mean?"

"I haven't noticed," I said honestly.

"Well, next time we're all together, watch. I

really want your honest opinion, Krista," she said with a worried look on her face. "I talked to Cathy in gym the other day. And I told her about how we might be forming a band. So anyway, I asked her if she'd watch Lou during orchestra and see if he looked interested in me. . . ."

"And?" I prompted.

Her voice came out sounding wistful. "She said that she honestly hadn't noticed anything different so far, and that he seemed to be really into his music during orchestra. But she agreed to start watching him whenever she sees us talking, or whatever." Ter was running a finger along the seam of her jeans. "That's why I need your input too," she said, looking up at me.

I nodded slowly.

"I don't know," she continued. "Maybe it's just too early for him to like me like I want him to," she said stalwartly.

"Right," I agreed.

The next day after school, I was doing some research for economics in the county library. I had two reference books and four periodicals laid out on in front of me. And I needed to find even more information. I'm not very interested in economics—except maybe my own personal economics. I didn't care much about international trade or the trade deficit. If countries wanted to get themselves into monetary trouble by importing too little or exporting too much, that was their problem. But unfortunately my teacher, Mr. Hernandez, felt differently. He had assigned us a heavy-duty ten-page paper, and I was desperately trying to get enough information to write an intelligent-sounding report.

I rose from my seat and headed for the book stacks again. I rounded the end of the aisle, moving toward the shelves where I knew my next source would be, but I found my feet stumbling over themselves. Lou was standing right in front of the spot I'd been aiming for. He turned his head and looked at me, his eyebrows rising in surprise. Then he smiled.

I walked up to him and noticed he was holding the book I needed. "Hey, that's the book I wanted," I said. "You have economics with Hernandez, too?"

"Yup."

"So do I," I said. "First period."

"Good for you," he said. "At least you get it over with right away."

"Oh yeah? Try concentrating on that stuff at 7:55 in the morning," I said, laughing. "I'm practically inert at that hour. My brain doesn't wake up until third period."

"But being unconscious for Hernandez's class sounds ideal," he said. "I'm wide awake by the time I have to face him during fifth."

"Ugh, right after lunch," I said with appropriate sympathy. "It must give you heartburn."

We grinned at each other.

"So did Hernandez assign your class a ten-page treatise?" I asked.

"Yeah, we got the monster report to do, too," I answered. "Which is why I'm here at the library instead of where I really want to be—home practicing my drums."

"Me, too, although for me it would be violin," I said, looking down at the book he was clutching under his arm. "You know, I really need that book." I tried to put on a winsome, begging expression.

Lou laughed. "I'll make you a deal," he said, holding the book aloft. "As soon as I photocopy the pages I need in here, I'll let you have it."

"Fair enough," I said, satisfied.

I returned to my seat and started scribbling some notes from the sources I had already amassed around me. Lou returned to his own table and sat down with his back facing me. I stared at his wide, strong-looking shoulders, and the weights in his garage came to mind. Then I reminded myself firmly that I was in the library to study economics, not human anatomy.

Twenty minutes later Lou appeared at my elbow and laid the book down next to me. "All done," he said, juggling a sheaf of photocopies. "Good luck understanding this stuff."

"That bad, huh?" I asked, smiling up at him.

"Worse." He grinned and went back to his table. This time he sat down facing in my direction.

I tried to go back to my reading, but I felt slightly distracted. I tipped my head down, making my long blond hair fall in a sheer curtain partially covering my face, and looked across at him. I had discovered early on in my life that this was an extremely useful maneuver, because it allowed me to watch people without them knowing. Lou seemed to be staring at me, but I tried to convince myself that I was imagining things. Maybe he was just mulling over an economics problem. For a long time, though, or so it seemed. I frowned and prodded my pen into action, writing gibberish. I wiggled in my seat. I aligned my paper more neatly, then pressed on the pages of the book spread open in front of me to make it lie flatter. Lou was still pondering—and staring at my table. I looked down at my book again and tried to read it, but the print on the pages blurred, and the words made no sense to me. This was ridiculous. There *had* to be an easier book about the common market.

I got up, scurried down the aisle, and replaced

the book. I chose another one that had larger print. I figured that if the print was larger, it would be easier to understand. Then I returned to my table.

I sat down facing away from Lou, knowing full well that I was being ridiculous. The guy had every right to stare anywhere he wanted. We were separated by at least twenty feet, and the library was full of other tables at which several people sat doing whatever they were doing. At twenty feet it was certainly possible that I couldn't focus well enough to really know where Lou's eyes were aimed. The fact that I had perfect vision meant nothing. People with excellent vision make mistakes all the time. Look at how three different people can witness an accident and not tell the same story.

Suddenly I sensed a presence nearby and shifted my eyes away from my book. Lou loomed large next to me for the second time.

"I'm out of here," he said. "There's just so much of this torture I can take." He was grinning down at me. His eyes were the color of bittersweet chocolate.

"Uh, okay. Bye," I said, hoping he would think I'd been staring at economics books so long my brain cells had liquefied.

"See you tomorrow night, right?"

I struggled to remember why. "Oh, yeah," I

said, bobbing my head up and down. "The jam session. It'll be great." I tried to infuse sufficient enthusiasm into my voice. What was my problem anyway?

I saw a flicker of a frown on his face, then his expression cleared, and he smiled. "Yeah, great," he said. "Catch you later." He nodded and sauntered off. I made myself look down at my book, and restrained myself from watching him go.

A weird feeling sat in my chest, making me feel uncomfortable, uneasy. I'd never felt anything like it before, so I couldn't identify it. But I hated the feeling. I bit my tongue and realized that I'd been grinding my teeth. I grabbed up my pen, yanked the book closer to me, and forced myself to copy several pages of information. I could have just photocopied what I needed, but I thought that by doing mindless busywork I might somehow shake whatever it was that was making me feel so tense.

"I stopped off at Tape World last night and bought us some sheet music," Ter was telling the three of us the next day.

We were all standing outside the orchestra room just before class. I tried not to look at Lou, even though he was standing directly across from me. I hoped that if I didn't make eye contact with him, he wouldn't mention seeing me in the library the day before. There was no reason Ter shouldn't know I had run into Lou. So why hadn't I just mentioned it to her offhandedly while we were driving to school that morning?

"Great," Scott said, beaming. "What did you get?"

"It's a surprise," Ter answered, her eyes shining. "I'll show you later."

"Tease," Scott joked.

Then we heard Mr. Marsh yelling for order.

"We'd better get in there before he blows a gasket," Scott said.

We all traipsed in and took our places. But just before I sat down, I happened to glance up at the drum section behind us. Lou was looking in Ter's and my direction, but for a second I felt his glance lock with mine. Then his eyes shifted off to the side by a fraction, and he winked. That's when I realized Ter had been looking at him too.

I didn't look at Ter once we had turned around and taken our seats, but I could hear her humming a little tune under her breath. Had Lou been staring at me? Or Ter? And if he'd been looking at me, why?

I shook my head and turned my attention to my violin. Mr. Marsh has an impossible dream:

He wants our orchestra to play like the Philadelphia Orchestra. He had even given us the score for *The Nutcracker* and had actually expected us to play it at the winter concert. No one in class had the heart to tell him that the likelihood of that happening was close to nil, so we practiced like fiends for forty minutes each day. And when the period was over, I think all of us just wanted to lie down and take naps.

After class, Cathy came up from behind me. "He must think we're all candidates for Julliard," she whispered.

I clucked with my tongue. "Poor misguided man," I said.

"Really. What does he expect? This is only the second week of school," Gavin said, joining us.

Dan overheard us from his place right next to mine. "If we improved our attitudes, instead of being defeatist like *some* people, maybe we *could* play like we were in Julliard."

I clenched my jaw and started packing up my violin with slow, methodical motions, hoping he would get out of my sight before my baser instincts took over.

Ter made a growling noise deep in her throat. "Some day Daniel Nguyen is going to find that violin rammed down his throat," she said under her breath.

Cathy and Gavin laughed.

"What's so funny?" Jojo asked, tramping down from her position up in the risers. As Ter gave her an account of Dan's latest remarks, Scott appeared at my side.

"So, you guys coming over now?" he asked. On our lunch break, we had agreed to practice for a couple of hours after school before I went to work.

"Absolutely," I said, still smiling at the picture of Dan with a violin in his throat.

"Great!" Scott said. "Then let's get out of here."

"What are you guys up to?" Gavin asked.

Before either Ter or I could say anything, Scott responded. "It's a secret," he said, raising his eyebrows and placing a forefinger over his lips. Then he grabbed me and pulled me out of the huge room. Ter and Lou followed right behind us, and we ran like gazelles over to the senior lockers.

"Why did you tell him that?" I asked Scott, gasping for breath.

"'Cuz I don't want anyone to know about our band until we sound really good," he explained.

"Oh," I said in response. But I really wanted to point out that we *did* sound good together. Scott had said so himself. How good did we have to sound before we could tell people about our band? I wondered. Then I realized Gavin would probably find out about the band very soon anyway, through his sister Cathy, whom Ter had told, but I decided that there was no point in mentioning that to Scott.

After whipping out what we needed from our lockers, we continued on to the parking lot, where Lou jumped into Scott's Jeep, and I hopped into Ter's car. Ter kept up a constant stream of chatter all the way to Lou's. I hadn't seen her this happy in months. She's in love, I thought, smiling, but then I felt an uneasiness settle somewhere deep in my chest once again.

The music Ter had bought us was *Tell It Like It Is,* from Heart.

"This is for girls' voices," Scott objected.

"So adapt," Ter said, wrinkling her nose at him.

Scott cocked his head to one side and gave me a warm full smile. "Come on, Krista, come on over here. I'll try this song with you."

I came over and read the music with him. Then we ran through the song a couple of times. Scott said we sounded great, then he announced that Lou had a surprise for us too.

Lou looked pink from embarrassment, but Scott went on anyway. "Here it is," Scott an nounced, waving some sheet music over his head. "Lou's original composition.

"You wrote something?" Ter all but squealed.

Lou just grinned.

"That's great, Lou," I said, taking the music from Scott. "I had no idea you could write music." I quickly skimmed over the pages. There were no lyrics. It was a straight instrumental piece.

"He'll be the next John Lennon," Scott said, looking at Lou with undisguised admiration.

We practiced the piece, and found that it had some great sound combinations. It started out slow, built up to a fast pace, then subsided into a sustained moderate pace. And Lou had allowed for each one of us to have solos, too. We practiced the song for about half an hour, before Scott suggested that we call it a day. "We sound so good, I don't want to spoil it," he said.

We laughed, feeling elated, and packed up our instruments. Then Lou led us into his house where we had snacks. I was beginning to realize that this was standard procedure for the guys. Music first, then snacks.

Lou's dog, Doglette, came into the living room where we were hanging out. She went around the room, sitting in front of each of us, trying to beg. Predictably, Ter gave in first. She put a piece of pepperoni on the carpet, and Doglette nosed it around the room, trying to figure out if she wanted to eat it or play with it. We watched her and laughed, until Lou took the dog and the pepperoni and threw them both out into the backyard.

I glanced at my watch.

"Late?" Ter asked. She knew I had to be at work at six.

"Kind of," I answered. "But we have a few minutes." I knew Ter didn't want to go yet. She was sitting very close to Lou on his couch, and he had his arm stretched out behind her. Ter was feeding Lou chips and dip, and Scott sat at my feet with his back leaning up against my chair. I was very conscious of the way his right shoulder was touching my left leg.

"What nights do you work?" Lou asked me.

"Normally, Tuesday, Wednesday, and Friday nights," I replied. "But occasionally Ernesto asks me to fill in for someone who can't make it."

Lou nodded. "So what nights do you work *ab*normally?" he asked with a straight face.

"Huh?" I said, genuinely confused. Then I understood the joke, and we all laughed.

For some reason Lou's eyes lingered on me after the laughter had died down, and I felt uncomfortable. I quickly leaned over to face Scott. "You work too, right?"

He nodded vigorously.

"Where? When?"

"Oh, I work at a farm south of here on the mesa, where they grow trees, bushes, flowers, stuff like that," he replied. "A lot of the builders around here use our stuff to landscape lots in their subdivisions." He flexed his arm. "It's good healthy outdoor work, for strengthening muscles," he added heartily. "The better for playing a guitar."

I laughed, then reached up and felt his arm at the elbow. "Really? Well, you don't work enough," I teased. "There's a lot of bone here."

Scott chuckled, then grabbed my hand and held it.

"You mean the one north of Nipomo?" Ter said, perking up.

"Yeah," he said, looking surprised.

Ter went on. "My dad has his own land-scaping business. He buys stuff from that place."

"Yeah, we sell at a discount to landscapers," Scott said.

"I've been there a couple of times with him, to pick stuff up." Ter leaned forward, biting her lip. "What days do you work?" she asked.

"Every other Saturday, and Monday, Wednesday, and Thursday afternoons," he answered. "It's a real grind, but I need the cash to romance beautiful blondes." He grinned at me.

I laughed, trying to make light of his comment, but I knew Scott was only half joking. He really was interested in me, and knowing that made me nervous. I wasn't sure I was *as* interested in him.

I wondered why Ter was being so inquisitive

about Scott's job, but then I saw the **gleam** in her eye as she looked at me, and I knew she'd asked about it for my benefit. She was plotting some way for us to join her father one day when he went down to the mesa for a pickup.

Ter turned her attention to Lou. "Where do you work?" she asked, playing dumb. We both knew exactly where Lou worked, but Ter wasn't about to let him know that.

"My dad owns the Quick Stop market in Pismo," he offered. "I help him whenever he needs me. It's a bummer, though, because I never really know what my schedule's going to be. But at least he pays well," he added.

Ter listened to him, somehow managing to keep a straight face.

Then Lou suddenly grinned. "And Scott's not the only one who needs muscles," he said. "My dad makes me do everything that requires a lot of strength, so I have to keep in shape."

"Well, you're doing a fabulous job of that," Ter said with a sigh and an admiring look at Lou.

"Thanks," Lou said, smiling at her a bit awkwardly. He had a kindly smile, I decided. Somehow it didn't fit his physique, but it did suit his personality.

I glanced over at the grandfather clock on the other side of the room, and stood up from my chair. "I have to go," I announced.

Ter and the two guys rose from their seats, and we all walked out to Ter's car.

"Well, since we're all working tomorrow," Scott said, "when should we get together again to practice?"

Ter's detail-oriented brain kicked in immediately. Pointing to each of us in turn, she said, "Krista works tomorrow and Friday, but she has Thursday and Saturday off. Scott works tomorrow, but he has to work Thursday too. I work tomorrow and Friday, but I have Saturday off. So, unless Lou or Scott has to work Saturday, Saturday looks like the best bet."

"Amazing," Scott said, shaking his head. He looked at me and nodded toward Ter. "Is she on the honor roll or what?"

Ter beamed.

"Well, I've got Saturday off," Lou said.

"And I work Saturday in the daytime, but I have the night off," Scott said. "So we'll play Saturday night, okay?"

We all agreed, then Scott opened the car door for me. "Good night," he said softly. Then he leaned forward and gave me a light kiss on the lips.

I got into the car with Ter, and she drove me to work, singing, "Saturday night, Saturday night . . ."

seven

I stood on the shoulder of the highway, staring into the trunk of my father's car as if it were uncharted territory. I remembered all those times my father had said, "Krista, come outside with me and let me show you how to change a tire." And I had always come up with some kind of excuse. "I can't, I'm late for work," I'd say. Or "Oh, Dad, can't we do that tomorrow?" If it were physically possible, I would be kicking myself in the rear right now, I thought, staring at the spare tire. I knew it had to come out of the trunk, but I wasn't sure what was supposed to happen next.

Then a vehicle approached from behind and slowed down as it passed. I peered around the open trunk lid and saw a battered pickup truck pull over to the side, in front of my car. There was something vaguely familiar about the truck, but I wasn't sure where I had seen it. I just hoped it wasn't some crazy who saw his chance to take advantage of a "damsel in distress". I quickly looked into the trunk, searching for something to use as a weapon, though I couldn't help but laugh at my paranoia.

The sound of the pickup's door slamming shut made me look up. It was Lou! I stared at him in surprise as he ambled over to me, a grin on his face.

"Krista!" he said as he approached. "At first I didn't know who the blonde standing by this car was. This is a 1969 Monte Carlo." He made the observation in suitably awed tones, and ran a hand worshipfully over a gleaming black fender. I stood by and patiently watched him walk all the way around the car, his eyes taking in every detail. I'm used to this kind of reaction to my father's car.

"It's in *mint* condition," he said, his eyes still focused on the car. Then he looked at me. "Yours?"

"No. My father's," I answered. "I still haven't earned enough money to get my Toyota fixed, so I'm borrowing this to get to work." I glanced anxiously at my watch. "And I'm late. Ernesto is going to fry me like a chimichanga."

Lou burst out laughing. "Fry you like a chimi-changa?" he repeated. "I like that."

"Well, it's no joke," I said, smiling. "I've got to get going."

Lou sobered, then crouched down next to the flat. "Well, first we have to get the jack on."

"The jack," I repeated as if I were learning a foreign language.

"Yeah." Lou stood and walked over to my trunk. In about two seconds he had the spare out of the trunk and a bent piece of metal in his hand. He then took out some other contraption and proceeded to haul the stuff over to the defective tire. "Put the emergency brake on and then come watch. I'll show you how it's done," he said.

Somehow the prospect of having Lou guide me through changing a flat was immensely more appealing than having my father teach me. I put the emergency brake on, then joined him by the tire.

"First of all," he began, "you shouldn't jack the car all the way up until you've loosened the lug nuts."

"Oh," I said as if that made a lot of sense. But then I asked, "Lug nuts?"

He pointed at some knobby things on the tires. "Lug nuts," he said again. He fitted a tool over the hexagon-shaped things and wrenched all the nuts loose. "Then after all the nuts are loose, you jack up the car," he went on, working as he spoke.

"Oh, I didn't know that," I said. *Of course you didn't,* I yelled at myself. *If you had, you would have done it by now.* "It's a good thing you came along," I said inanely.

Lou grinned at me. "Isn't it?"

He returned to the task, and while he worked, I stared at him unabashedly. He was wearing a fitted white T-shirt, and those muscles he worked so hard on were now hard at work. His biceps pulled and wrenched, straining the sleeves of his shirt. Then I looked down at his legs, which were bent into a squatting position. Under his jeans, they looked nicely shaped and strong.

Suddenly an image of Scott popped into my mind—tall, slender, strong. But strong in a different way—maybe an inferior way, some traitorous part of my mind suggested. I squashed the thought and tore my gaze away from Lou's incredible body to stare at the ice plant along the highway. It wasn't much to look at, but I had to stare at something other than the guy my best friend was after.

Lou jacked up the car and pulled the flat off. "It's a good thing you don't have a donut," he said as he rolled the tire toward the trunk.

"A donut?" I asked, thoroughly confused. "What's food got to do with it?"

Lou attempted to hold back his laughter, but he couldn't stop himself from bursting out into hysterics. When he finally sobered, he forced himself to speak in a serious tone. "Not an eating donut. A small tire called a donut. It's rubber, black . . ." He lost his composure again, but managed to roll the spare tire over to the wheel well.

Lou positioned the spare in the axle, all the while explaining to me what he was doing. I tried to concentrate as he went on about the fascinating intricacies of tire replacement. But my eyes were focusing on the fascinating intricacies of his hair, his ears, his eyes, his . . . *Stop it!* a voice yelled from somewhere inside me.

Lou stood up and turned his bright smile on me. He dusted his hands on his hips. "There. All done," he said.

All done in, is more like it, I thought, feeling like a wrung-out cleaning cloth. "Thanks," I said to him inadequately. I was still staring at him. I couldn't help it. And *he* was looking right back at me.

"So, you come here often?" he quipped.

I smiled, finally relaxing a little. "Nope. First

time," I said. "So what were you doing out here?" I asked, trying to sound casual.

Lou pretended to look around furtively. "Don't tell my dad," he said. "But sometimes I visit a Mexican grocery store up in SLO when I need things he doesn't carry."

"Like what?" I asked.

"Fresh cilantro and flour tortillas."

I screwed up my face. "Cilantro. What's that?"

He shrugged. "It's a kind of a herb. Scott's dropping by after work and I'm making us dinner."

"So what are you cooking tonight?" I asked, trying to sound unfazed by his statement. I really wasn't used to hearing guys talk about cooking and grocery shopping.

"Enchiladas," he said with gusto. "Shredded beef mixed with my special sauce," he explained, his eyes lighting up with excitement. "I add a little of this and a little of that—" he said, waving his arms around, "then I stuff the filling in tortillas, smother them in more sauce, pile on the Monterey Jack, and bake them. Man, I'm hungry just thinking about it."

"You mean you just make up this recipe as you go along?" I asked in amazement. "You don't use a cookbook?"

Lou stepped backward dramatically. His dark

brows lowered over his eyes, and he asked, "Are there cookbooks? Really?"

I laughed, thinking of my mother who would probably not approve of Lou's style of cooking. "If you don't follow a recipe, Krista, how will you achieve the exact same results every time?" she tells me.

"Yeah, really," I said and glanced at my watch. Then I groaned. "I've really got to get to work," I said. "I'm running extra late today because I had to run out and buy a diet soda for my mother before leaving the house. She didn't think she'd make it through the night if she had to wait until after I got off work," I said with a shake of my head. "She lives on that stuff."

"Why? She's built like a chopstick," Lou remarked, looking puzzled.

I laughed. "Yeah, I know. But that's because she's always watching her weight."

I noticed Lou's eyes move up and down my body.

"Uh . . . Ter's always dieting, too," I found myself saying for no discernible reason.

"Well, she's doing a good job," Lou said.

For a minute we just stood there like idiots, staring at each other. Cars continued to zip by. *Zoom. Chug, chug, chug. Whine.* Each car had a distinct sound. And I realized my heart had suddenly acquired a new sound of its own:

thump, a-thump, thump. It beat in syncopated rhythm, far from its normal timing, and my chest felt as if it were too small to hold it. Then my lungs didn't seem able to fill to capacity. "Thanks for your help," I said and was shocked to hear how husky my voice had suddenly turned.

"De nada," Lou said softly.

The air between us suddenly seemed inadequate, as if we were both using way too much oxygen. He was looking at me intently and was standing so close that my view of the roadside was blocked out by his incredible broad shoulders. I've always hated guys obsessed with bodybuilding. But Lou's muscles were working muscles, not show muscles, so they seemed so much more . . . *sexy.*

"Well, I hope you don't get fried like a chimichanga," Lou said, reminding me of why I was even on the highway.

"Oh, God," I said and looked back at the car frantically. "I—I'm sorry. I have to run." I backed away to my car.

"Hey, don't apologize," he called after me. "I gotta go too. Scott'll be at my house in an hour." He smiled. "Just calm down. And drive safely."

He started to walk away, and I put out a hand and steadied myself on the top of my father's car. My knees felt as if they might give at any moment. After a couple of deep breaths, I wrenched open the passenger-side door, fell into the seat, remembered I was the driver, and scooted sideways behind the wheel. I looked up and saw Lou hopping into his truck.

Somehow I managed to get back into the flow of traffic. As I glided past Lou's pickup, I honked and waved a hand out the window. He honked back, then pulled in behind me. I was relieved when he got off at the next exit. I didn't want to have the distraction of watching him in my rearview mirror all the way to San Luis. I was still feeling a bit dazed from the encounter, and I needed to concentrate on the road.

I shook my head and tried to focus, but my mind kept wandering back to the image of Lou's arms, his eyes, his shoulders . . . *No!* I told myself. *I have to stop myself from falling for him. He's Ter's.*

The band met in Lou's garage the following Saturday night. I hadn't mentioned meeting Lou on the highway to either Scott or Ter, and as far as I could tell, Lou hadn't said anything about having run into me either.

I told myself that it was better to just forget about the whole encounter. I didn't want Ter to worry about something when she had absolutely nothing to worry about. Besides, if Lou saw no reason to mention the incident, *I* certainly didn't want to place undue emphasis on it.

Practice went well. Scott and I sang together, and he did some incredible stuff on his electric guitar. Fuzz tones. Reverberations. He was wonderful, and I could see that he had real talent. Maybe his dreams of going professional weren't so crazy after all.

After a couple of hours of playing, we plotted out our schedules for the following week. Ter took over as secretary and came up with two days we could all practice. Then Scott suggested that the four us spend the following Saturday at the beach.

"We'll ride the dunes in my Jeep," he said, getting up from his seat.

"Fabulous!" Ter said. "Krista and I will pack a picnic lunch."

"Good. I can have a day off from the kitchen," Lou joked. "I was getting dishpan hands from scrubbing all those pots."

Ter laughed and hugged him around the waist. Lou was laughing too, and he threw an arm around her shoulder.

"It's settled then," Scott said, giving me a big kiss on the cheek. I blushed, feeling uncomfortable with his affection. I couldn't figure out what was wrong with me. Here was a really nice guy who obviously liked me a lot . . . but I couldn't seem to make myself return the feeling.

During one of our practice sessions the next week, Scott announced that his father had agreed to let him put up a sign at his shop advertising the band.

"This will be our first real move toward getting some gigs," he said, smiling. "But of course, we'll have to come up with a name first." He looked around at all of us.

Then we started brainstorming for a catchy name. Ter said something about light and dark chocolate, which nobody took seriously. Scott suggested Us 2 in a takeoff of U2. Then Lou came up with California Dreamers, which I liked—but Scott thought it was too sweet. In the end, we decided to go home and work on it. Our homework was to bring lists of names to the next practice session.

That night, I sat in my room, staring at the wall, trying to come up with a name. For a long time, I couldn't come up with a thing. Then suddenly an idea popped into my mind: Heart Breakers. Hey, that's a pretty good name, I thought. But then I began to realize *why* I had thought of that name, and I quickly shoved it out of my mind.

eight

By the following Saturday I decided I should ignore the increasingly familiar dark feeling I was experiencing deep inside. Ter wanted Lou to like her in the worst way. And Scott seemed to like me a lot. I knew I should be thrilled that a guy like Scott was interested in me. Probably a dozen girls had crushes on him. So *what* if my heart didn't jump with excitement when I saw him? No boy had ever inspired that reaction in me before, so why should I expect it to happen this time? Besides, Ter was really counting on me. If I stopped seeing Scott now, I'd be breaking up the nice little group we four had become, and her chances of becoming Lou's girlfriend might somehow suffer because of it.

The guys picked us up at Ter's house. I'd stayed overnight there so Ter and I could spend the morning preparing the picnic lunch. We'd really made an effort to prepare foods we thought would appeal to them. Ter's little brother, Ricardo, told us what guys liked to eat: "Chocolate cake," he had said. "That's all you need." When we pressed him further, he finally admitted that hero sandwiches weren't too bad. So we made monster heroes, packed slabs of chocolate cake, and cans of soda. We threw in healthy stuff, too, like celery and carrot sticks and fruit, knowing full well that no one would touch them.

The guys arrived at noon, and Ter jumped into the back of the Jeep with Lou and the cooler. Scott had taken off the canvas and plastic top of his Jeep, and we rode down Grande Avenue and out onto Pismo State Beach in the open air. The wind blew through my hair so that it flapped around behind me, so I tied a scarf around my head and lifted my face to the sun.

It was a perfect beach day—deep blue sky, warm golden sun, waves rolling in, surf pounding, and miles of miles of dunes to explore. Scott handled his Jeep like a maniac, cresting one dune after another and kicking up a sandy spray behind us.

After about forty minutes of riding the dunes, we found a secluded area to stop at and have lunch. We spread out a huge beach blanket on the sand, and Ter and I passed around the overstuffed heroes we'd prepared. Judging by the way the guys bit into them, I'd say Ricardo's advice was right on the nose.

Out on the ocean we could see a few figures in wet suits. It looked as if they were trying to surf, but the waves were too small and petered out way before hitting the beach.

Patting his stomach in satisfaction, Scott lay back on the blanket and closed his eyes. "Man, this is the way to spend a Saturday," he said in a lazy voice.

"You got it, compadre," Lou said, leaning back on his arms and staring around him in satisfaction. Then he suddenly got an impish look on his face, and before either Ter or I knew what was happening, Scott and Lou were rolling all over the sand, wrestling. Ter squealed and jumped off the blanket, grabbing the remnants of her lunch. Sand was flying everywhere, and I was laughing so hard that my sides were starting to hurt.

"Man, we haven't done that since you lived with us," Lou said after everyone had settled down.

"You lived with Lou?" Ter asked, surprised.

"Yeah," Scott said. "Back in seventh grade. My parents were in a big car accident then, and they both ended up in the hospital with pretty serious injuries."

I was listening to him intently. This was the first I had ever heard of this.

Scott went on. "So anyway, the Pachecos let me come live with them until my parents got out of the hospital."

"How long was that?" I asked.

"Just a couple of weeks. But it was wild," he said, looking at Lou. "Three of us were crammed in one room, and I slept on a mattress on the floor next to Lou's bed. It was crazy—like living in a bachelor's dorm." He chuckled. "Remember those wrestling matches we had?"

Lou nodded. "It's a miracle we survived those," he said.

"Yeah," Scott agreed. "Roberto could be so manic."

"Roberto's your older brother, right?" Ter asked.

"Yeah," Lou answered shortly.

After that, both of the guys clammed up. Lou stared out at the ocean, and Scott began rummaging through the cooler. I didn't know what was going on, but I was fairly certain that it was the subject of Roberto that made them feel uncomfortable. I looked across at Ter.

She seemed tense too, and she was biting her lower lip.

At that moment a dog came bounding down the beach. We could see he was aiming for a Frisbee a man had thrown. He leaped into the air, caught it cleanly, and ran back toward his master. We laughed, watching the antics of the dog a couple of minutes, and then Scott said, "You know who that dog reminds me of?"

"Yeah," Lou said. I thought there was a catch to his voice. "Hound Dog."

"Hound Dog?" Ter prompted.

Lou smiled at her. "Yeah, up to a year ago I had this dog I named Hound Dog. Man, that dog was something else. He could chase a Frisbee just like that one."

"Or anything else you threw," Scott said with evident admiration.

"Right. An old shoe, a rock, it didn't matter," Lou said, laughing.

"What happened to him?" I asked.

"Oh, he got old and sick," Lou explained, scooping up a handful of sand and letting it sift through his fingers. "He was part shepherd and part malamute . . . a really handsome guy. But then he got arthritis, which crippled him. And they said he was also suffering from the beginnings of kidney failure, and that the only thing we could do was—" He swallowed. "You know, put him to sleep."

"Oh, no!" Ter said, gasping.

Lou looked at Scott, his expression a combination of affection and sadness. "Remember that day?"

"Yeah," he said solemnly. "We decided to take him to the beach one last time, and he was so weak, he could only lie down in the back of my Jeep."

I swallowed.

"He used to stand up back there, tail and tongue flying in the wind. But that last day he didn't even look over the side once," Scott continued with obvious difficulty. "He just lay there, panting, as if he could barely breathe."

"Do you think he knew what was coming?" Lou asked. His eyes were shining like polished pieces of coal.

"I don't know. I really hope not," Scott said sadly.

"Anyway," Lou said, taking a deep breath, "when we got him out on the beach, he just sat there. And that's when I knew I just had to do it. . . ."

I glanced at Ter and saw that she was wiping at her eyes.

"Man, were we messes that day," Scott said, his voice tight. "We cried like babies."

"So is Doglette a replacement?" I asked, immediately regretting the words as soon as they left my mouth.

"No," Lou said firmly. "You can't replace a dog. That's what I told Scott when he kept bugging me about getting another dog." He looked up and grinned at his friend.

"Bugging you!" Scott yelped. "Yeah, well," he admitted, "but aren't you glad I did?"

Lou chuckled. "You were a pain in the neck!"

"That's what friends are for," Scott said.

They grinned at each other, and I realized then that these guys had a friendship that equaled Ter's and mine. And that surprised me. I had never witnessed that kind of intimacy between two male friends, and I hadn't really expected it for some reason.

"Doglette's a weird name," Ter said. "How did you come up with that?"

Lou's face immediately brightened. "After Scott convinced me that I needed another dog to help me heal, we went to the shelter in Santa Maria—just this past June. And we saw this cute puppy, a cross between a shepherd and a collie. The people there claimed it would turn out to be a big dog." Lou laughed as if he were recalling the scene. "Man, that puppy was tiny. So I said to them, 'That's not a dog. That's a doglette.' And the name stuck!"

We all laughed, but then fell into silence once again. I think Ter must have been afraid the mood would turn somber again, because I could detect the panic in her eyes.

"So you guys have known each other a long time?" she asked.

"Yeah," Lou said, smiling at Scott. "Too long."

"Very cute, amigo," Scott returned, punching Lou in the arm.

Then Lou looked at Ter and me. "And how long have you two known each other?"

"Since second grade," Ter said, looking at me fondly. "We met one day during recess. Two boys from the third grade were picking on me."

I smiled and nodded as I remembered that day.

"I was little for my age and that probably didn't help," Ter went on. "Anyway, they were white guys, and they were making remarks about me, saying I didn't have any right to live in this country . . . that my parents were wetbacks."

"Aaagh!" Lou spat out in disgust, and I realized he must have been familiar with that sort of discrimination on a personal level.

"Yeah," Ter said, nodding at Lou. "But Krista had been playing with some girls nearby, and she'd been watching the whole thing. So when one of the guys shoved me down into the dirt, she ran over, yelling at them. 'Her parents do not have wet backs!' she said, and then she threatened to punch their lights out."

We broke into laughter at the story, then Scott looked at me. "What were you, the class bully?" he asked.

I smiled. "No, but at that time, I was the tallest person in the class," she said. "I figured my size would scare them away. I had no idea what wetbacks were, but it didn't matter. I just hated to see them pick on someone else, and it worked. They left Ter alone."

"Yeah, and after that I started to hang around Krista," Ter said.

"And we started to get to know each other. . . . I mean, I couldn't just ignore this little girl who was always following me around," I said, shrugging and aiming a teasing look at Ter.

She wrinkled her nose at me, but smiled.

After that the four of us talked a little bit more about names for our band, but we were really having difficulty agreeing on anything. So finally Scott jumped up, pulled me to my feet, and said, "Let's go for a walk."

We started down the beach, leaving Lou and

114

Ter behind on the blanket. Scott held my hand as we walked.

"I've been looking at college catalogs, trying to figure out which ones have the best music departments," Scott said. "I figure if I have to go, then at least I'll pick one where I can work toward a career in music."

"Sounds reasonable to me," I said.

"Yeah, but my parents just don't understand how serious I am about being a musician," he said. "They think I'll forget all about it once I get to college."

"Why don't they want you to be a musician?"

"Because there's no guarantee I'll make it," he explained. "They think I'm doomed to a miserable life if I pursue music. But I know I'm going to make it!" he said fiercely. "I'm not that easily defeated." Then he grinned and squeezed my hand. "Move over, Eric Clapton," he said with a laugh.

I smiled. "I know how it feels to not have your parents behind you one hundred percent," I said pensively. "That's the way it is with my parents sometimes. My dad's a builder, and my mom's the executive loan officer at the Intercostal Bank—very serious careers," I said, grinning. "And they can't seem to relate to my interests either."

"Which are?"

"Well, have you ever heard of professional storytellers?"

"Writers, you mean?"

"No, professional storytellers go around to schools and libraries to tell stories to kids," I explained. "I want to do that by telling stories on my guitar."

"Hmmm," Scott said, cocking his head to one side.

"We have someone who does that down at the county library from time to time, and I think it's so neat," I added.

Scott appeared interested. "What kind of stories do they tell?"

"Oh, folktales from different countries. Or sometimes they make up stories. Or they adapt stories from books," I said. "Storytellers help kids use their imaginations and make them want to read more."

"That's great," Scott said.

"Yeah. And I could use my music, too. A lot of folk songs tell tales."

"So that's how you want to use your music?"

"Yes—ideally. Only my parents feel like yours . . . they don't think I could ever earn a living that way." I scowled and added in a low voice, "They're probably right, too. That's why I'm going to major in English. If I go to a teacher's college, then at least I'll have school teaching to fall back on."

Scott frowned. "It seems like a rip-off that someone who plays and sings like you can't have a chance at making a career of it."

We walked a little farther without speaking. Then Scott said, "Maybe our band will be such a success that we'll prove everybody wrong. Maybe your parents and mine will take our music more seriously once we get our first gig." His voice was growing more animated as he spoke. "After we settle on a name, we should talk about whether or not we want costumes. Maybe we could dress all in black or something. . . ."

He continued to share his ideas about the band with me, but I didn't contribute much. Instead I just listened, feeling a little bit awed by his energy and the level of his enthusiasm.

Scott stopped walking about a mile down the beach, and pulled me close to him. He put his arms around my waist. "Krista, remember the first day of orchestra?" he asked, looking down at me.

I nodded.

"Well, when I saw you and Teresa come in that day, I just knew that I'd really like you. And I hoped that I could get to know you better." He paused for a moment and just looked at me. "I was right about you," he whispered. "You're really terrific. And . . . I've never met anyone like you before."

117

I stared at him. I didn't know what to say. And then he kissed me.

Scott's lips were warm and gentle. They didn't ask for more than I could give. But I was receiving a very clear message. Scott really, really liked me. I knew I didn't return the emotion to the same degree. And that made me feel guilty.

Scott pulled back and looked at me with so much warmth. As we walked, hand in hand, back toward Ter and Lou, I decided I didn't like myself very much. And I wondered how long I could keep pretending that I was comfortable with where our relationship was leading.

We joined Ter and Lou, who convinced us to go for a walk on the boardwalk, where there was a mini mall. So we all hopped into the Jeep and drove to an adjacent parking lot. After some window shopping, we came across a photo booth.

"Hey, let's get our pictures taken," Ter said. So all four of us piled in the booth, the guys sharing the seat and balancing Ter and me on their laps. We laughed and mugged and took two group shots. Then Scott suggested that each couple pose separately for the last two shots. So Lou and Ter leaped out of the booth just as the third flash went off, and then Scott and I quickly jumped out to let them sit for the last shot.

The guys let Ter and me have all four photos. She and I watched as Scott took out a pocket knife and cut the picture strip into four pieces. He handed me the one of us and gave the remainder to Ter. She was thrilled, of course, and she giggled as she tucked the photos away in her purse.

After playing a couple rounds of pinball in the arcade, we wandered back to the Jeep and prepared to head for home. The sun was low in the sky, just about to sink below the rim of the world. The air was already beginning to get chilly, and the fog bank out at sea was starting to move in closer. Scott and Lou wrestled the top back on the Jeep, and then we started toward home.

We drove to Ter's house first, and Lou walked her to the door. Scott's arm was wrapped around my shoulders, and I had my head pressed against his chest. From that angle, I had an excellent view of Lou and Ter on her front porch—and of the kiss they shared. I tried to focus my eyes on something else, but for some reason, I couldn't help but watch. I didn't know who was initiating the kiss, but it seemed to last a very long time. The dark, awful feeling I hated welled up inside me. I took deep breaths, but it wouldn't go away. I turned my head into Scott's chest and listened to his heart beating. It sounded normal to me, unlike my own, which was thumping so hard that I was sure Scott would feel it.

As soon as Ter was inside, Lou came back and leaped into the back of the Jeep. Scott put it in gear and drove with one hand, keeping me wrapped up in his other arm.

At my own front door I turned to say good night to Scott. Then I spotted Lou in the Jeep. Responding to a sudden impulse, I threw my arms around Scott's neck and pulled him tightly against me. Our kiss was longer than the one Ter and Lou had shared. I made sure of that. And when I finally pulled away from him, I noticed that he was breathing heavily and that he was looking at me strangely.

"Whew," he said, running a finger down the side of my check. "I can't wait to see you again." His voice was husky.

I fumbled for the door handle and practically fell into my house. "Good night," I said, knowing he'd think I was breathless from the kiss. But it was the horror of realizing why I had kissed him like that that had taken my breath away. I had wanted Lou to see it.

nine

In orchestra Monday I played my violin with more energy than usual. I pretended it was only me in the room and I concentrated solely on the music. I wanted to distract myself from thinking about Lou. And I wanted to forget that I was in danger of doing something that would hurt Ter. So I threw myself into the music, completely obliterating all other thoughts and feelings from my mind.

At the end of the period Dan turned to me and said, "Well, finally *someone* is giving one hundred percent." Then he packed up his violin and walked away.

"Was that supposed to be a compliment?" Cathy said, suddenly appearing at my side.

Jojo bounded down the risers and joined us. "Hey, how's the band going?" she asked me.

"Never mind the band," Cathy said, grinning. "How are the big romances going?"

"Shhh," Ter whispered, glancing around to see if Scott or Lou was close enough to hear.

"Everyone's talking about you guys," Cathy went on, sounding excited. "They see you four eating lunch together out on the quad. And everyone wants to know when we can hear you play."

"Uh . . ." I said, staring at her stupidly. The last thing I wanted to do was talk about the four of us, and I had an impulse to flee the room to get away from everyone.

"People are talking about what neat couples you guys make," Jojo said. "And Krista, you and Scott look *so* great together."

I forced a smile and busied myself by packing up my violin. "I have to get to work," I mumbled, hoping that sounded like a believable explanation for my lack of enthusiasm.

"Yeah, me too," Cathy said, sighing. Then her eyes shifted to a point somewhere behind me. "I think it's time for our exit, Jojo," she said. "Here come the guys!"

Jojo giggled, then discretely slipped away with Cathy.

The guys came over to walk Ter and me to our

lockers and then to the cars. Somehow I managed to smile and chat as though everything were normal. But inside me was a jumble of confusion. I had so many things to think about, so many emotions to sort out. And all I wanted to do was get away.

It took all my energy to pretend nothing was wrong. I said my good-byes to the guys and hopped into Ter's car without arousing any suspicion from anybody—not even Ter. I suppose she was too wrapped up in her excitement about Lou to notice I wasn't myself. All the way to my house, she talked about how great he looked, how wonderful he was, what he said at lunch . . .

It drove me crazy.

I decided I needed some space—away from Ter—to think. Being around her was getting more and more difficult. Every time she talked about Lou, I had this awful fear that I'd say something incriminating. Or that I'd react to something she said in such a way that she'd know I was attracted to him. So I decided that I should spend less time with her.

The first thing I needed to do was get my car fixed, which meant that I needed to work overtime to earn enough money. But once it was fixed, I wouldn't be dependent on Ter for transportation on the nights I couldn't borrow my father's car. Still, even if I did work more hours, it would take some time before I had saved up enough. My Toyota needed a new clutch, which would cost around $560, and so far I had saved up $415. That left a balance of $145, which translated to almost three weeks of work.

As it turned out, all Ernesto could give me was one more night a week—Sunday. And that was one of the few nights the band could get together and practice. So when I told Ter, Scott, and Lou about my new schedule, I tried to make it sound as if my parents were pushing me to get my car fixed sooner. They were all disappointed, of course, but nobody could come up with an alternative solution for me. So in the end, we decided to do our best and work around the new schedule.

About a week later, Scott engineered what he called an "official" date.

"Playing in Lou's garage doesn't count," he argued when I pointed out that we were together a lot already. "That's work, not entertainment. I want a *real* date. You know, so that we can all go somewhere dressed up in great clothes. Maybe we could go to a movie and then out to eat."

"You sound like a girl," I said, laughing.

"You sound like a boy," he shot back.

So after Scott got off work the following day, we all went to see the latest Kevin Costner movie.

Scott sat next to me on the aisle, with one arm around my shoulders and the other holding my hand. I was using my one free hand to feed popcorn into his mouth since, as he put it, he was slightly handicapped by not having a third arm. Lou sat beside me, and Ter sat on his other side. And I could see, using my peripheral vision, that Lou's arm was around Ter.

The popcorn lasted no more than five minutes into the movie, and then there was nothing to distract us except the film. I sat there staring at the screen. But I wasn't seeing any of the action. Instead I was obsessed with the fact that Lou was right next to me. And that his left leg was within two inches of my right leg. And that if for any reason he were to move those two inches, our legs would be touching. I was worried about how I'd react if his leg came in contact with mine.

I stole a glance at Ter, whose eyes were riveted on the screen. She let out a sob, and Lou promptly pulled out a tissue and handed it to her. Then as he settled back in his seat, the event I had feared occurred. His leg dropped over those two measly inches and landed right next to mine. We were joined from thigh to knee.

I did not jump at the contact. I did not pull away in shock. I did nothing.

And neither did Lou.

For the remainder of the movie I continued to stare straight up at the screen, completely oblivious to whatever I was seeing. I was wrapped up in a cocoon of emotions that clouded my vision and muddled my brain. Why didn't he break contact? Didn't he realize what had happened? *I* couldn't move away because I didn't want to seem as if I were overreacting to his touch. And on another level, I wanted to touch Lou. Badly.

I was jolted out of my stupor when the lights came on in the theater. I jumped from my seat and looked around frantically as if I'd just come out of a coma. Scott grabbed my hand and led me out of the theater. Then Lou and Ter came up behind us, and we stood outside in the cool night air.

"Was that a great movie, or *what*?" Scott said.

"It was," Ter said. "I've never seen anything that grabbed my attention so solidly. I thought my heart was going to break when they killed him."

Scott and Ter began an animated discussion of the highs and lows of the movie. I had absolutely nothing to add to the discussion, and I fervently hoped no one would ask me for my opinion. I absolutely could not remember what the movie had been about. I couldn't even have told you if it was a western, a sci-fi movie, or a drama.

And then I noticed the blank expression on Lou's face. But when he noticed me staring at him, a flush crept up his neck to his face. He suddenly shifted and turned away, looking at the people passing by, at the sky, at the marquee, at everything but me. What was he feeling? I wondered, and the question kept ringing in my ears until late that night when I lay, sleepless, in my bed.

I got very little sleep that night, and the next morning it was almost eleven by the time I emerged from my room. My parents were lounging in the family room, drinking coffee and reading the Sunday paper. They looked up at me as I moved sluggishly into the kitchen.

"What's the matter, Krista?" my mother asked. "I know it can't be that you stayed out too late last night. You came home by eleven."

"Uh . . ." I tried to think up a plausible excuse for not having slept much, but what could I say? "I'm just a little tired I guess," I said. "I have to go to work tonight and I just thought I'd sleep in."

My parents looked at me with concern. "I suppose you'll be needing the car?" my father said.

"Uh, yeah," I answered.

"Really, Krista," my mother said, lowering her newspaper. "I don't understand why you asked for an extra night just so you could get your car fixed sooner. I thought the arrangement you worked out with Teresa was just fine."

"Yeah, but I don't want to have to rely on her all the time," I mumbled. "She might want to have more freedom to do other things." Like be with Lou, I added silently. I wrenched the orange juice out of the fridge and poured myself a glass.

"Well, I think she *should* try to get her car serviced sooner," my father said. Then he looked at me. "Do you realize it's twenty-five miles to where you work, Krista? Why can't you get a transfer to the Taco Bell on Grande?"

I knew he was thinking of the mileage I was putting on his car. "Dad, that's not how it works. We're not talking about IBM, you know," I said. "And I thought about going to the Intercostal Bank and applying for a loan, but I didn't think the loan officer would approve my application." I gave my mother a mischievous smile.

Her mouth tightened, and I could practically hear the words my parents had chorused at me when I told them I wanted the car: "You better plan on paying its upkeep on your own. Foreign cars cost a lot more to fix."

My parents returned to reading the paper.

"I'm constantly amazed and disgusted by how much building went on while we were in Washington," my mother said, holding up the real estate section. "Every flat piece of acreage!"

"I don't know why you're disgusted," my father said in an amused tone. "I would think as a loan officer you'd be happy about all those extra mortgages. Surely they bring in more interest money for your bank."

She grimaced at him over the edge of the paper. "Yeah, it's great for the bank," she said. "But as a resident, I'm sick of it. This area has gotten so built up, I hardly recognize it anymore."

"At least the beach is the same," Dad said happily. He looked over to the breakfast bar where I was slouched over my juice. "By the way," he said, "your mother and I will be going for our usual run on the beach, then afterwards we're going to the Randalls for a cookout."

"Fine," I said, sounding depressed. "I'll think of you when I'm serving up burritos."

My mother's eyes sharpened on me. "I hope you aren't coming down with something, Krista. You don't sound like your usual self."

I got up and groped in the cabinet, pretending

129

to look for a cereal box. I was coming down with something all right, but I didn't think there was a medical cure for it.

Ter called at noon. She wanted to get together and talk about the previous night's date, but I begged off. I told her I wasn't feeling that great and that I was going to sit around and watch a movie and rest up for work. She seemed to understand, although I thought I heard a hurt tone in her voice. When I hung up, I realized she had probably hoped I'd invite her over to watch, too. In the past I always had.

I searched through the videos we kept in the house. I didn't really feel like watching anything, but being left alone with my own thoughts was a worse alternative. I scanned the tapes once again, and my hand paused over *Fiddler on the Roof,* a truly sad movie I wasn't sure I could handle. But for some reason I pulled out the two-tape box and put part one in the VCR. I watched fatalistically. Even though the movie starts out in a lighthearted tone, the last half gets pretty grim. I watched glassy eyed as the poor tailor appealed to his lover's father, saying that even a poor tailor deserved to find happiness. I clicked the movie off. True love had triumphed over a system that expected all marriages to be arranged. I thought about Scott and me and Ter and Lou. To some degree, I felt that the way we were coupled up was also arranged. I knew that Ter had made the decision about which guy I was to date—"You can have the Nordic type," she had said that first time we had seen them. And it seemed that Scott had made the choice for both of the guys. Scott had said that he liked me the first time he saw me, so I was willing to bet that he urged Lou to go after Ter. I wondered if Lou was happy with the choice that had been made for him.

As I was dressing for work, the phone rang.

"Hi, Krista," the voice said. "I'm glad I caught you at home."

"Oh, hi, Scott," I said.

"Man, you sound down," he said. "But then, I guess I'd sound that way too if I had to work on Sunday."

"Uh, yeah," I agreed quickly. "What's up?"

"Nothing much," he said. "I just called to tell you I was going to miss you tonight. I'm heading out to that party Gavin's throwing on the beach, and I wish you could come with me. But I guess you can't get out of work, huh?"

"Not after I asked to work extra," I said, trying not to show that I didn't actually care about the party. Though the party would probably be a lot of fun, I just didn't feel like going with Scott. The energy I'd need to pretend to like him as much as he liked me would be more than I felt able to muster.

"Yeah, that's what I thought. But I thought there'd be no harm in asking," he said cheerfully. "Well, I'll let you go now. I'll be thinking of you."

"Yeah," I choked out.

Oh, Scott, I thought miserably after I hung up. What am I going to do about you?

At work Ernesto asked if I could fill in for someone the very next night, which was a Monday. Since it wasn't a practice night, and since it would give me that many more dollars toward my goal, I agreed.

Ter was also working Monday night, but since she had to work right after school, and I didn't have to be at work until five, I had to borrow my father's car once again. He was not pleased when I came in and asked for it, but he handed me the keys and had my mother take him to work Monday morning.

So for the second time in two days, I found myself serving up burritos. Before I had started working for Taco Bell, I actually liked Mexican food. But now I was seriously thinking about applying to a Chinese restaurant. The smells of Mexican cooking were really beginning to make me sick.

I was just wondering what Chinese food would smell like when I turned to face the next customer . . . it was Lou! We both opened our mouths in surprise.

"I thought you didn't work on Mondays," he said.

"I don't. I'm just filling in for someone." My heart felt like it was going to leap out of my chest.

"Ah." He looked uncomfortable.

"How come you're way up here?" I asked.

"Well, my parents are both working, and Scott's busy, so I decided I'd grab a bite to eat on my way home," he explained.

"Home from where?" I asked curiously. I knew Scott was busy, and I wondered why Lou wasn't also at Gavin's beach party.

Lou's face fell, and he looked extremely uncomfortable. "Uh, I was just riding around," he said. It didn't sound as if that was the real explanation, but I kept my doubts to myself.

We stared at each other for a minute, and then the person standing in line behind Lou let out a cough.

"I'll take the taco dinner and a Coke," Lou said quickly.

I served him in record time, and he smiled at me before walking over to a table.

I took the next couple of orders, but could not control my eyes. They kept insisting on glancing at Lou. And two times out of three, when I looked his way, he was looking mine. Finally he finished eating and got up to throw his stuff in the trash. He strolled over to the counter and leaned against it. At the moment there wasn't anyone for me to wait on.

"So, when do you get off?" he asked.

"Ten."

"Oh." He kind of nodded his head in a vague gesture, then asked, "What's Teresa up to tonight?"

"She's probably home from work by now," I said, wondering why he didn't know that.

"Oh." He looked up at the wall behind me, then at a customer just coming up to the counter. "Well, see you tomorrow," he said, backing away.

"Yeah." I watched Lou leave, thinking to myself that it was strange he didn't know Ter's whereabouts. I watched his pickup exit the parking lot and head toward the freeway. Was he as interested in Ter as she was in him? His actions were impossible for me to read. Yet the way he acted sometimes made me think he might not be all that into her. Or maybe there was someone else? A vision of Ter's pained face immediately sprang to mind. I could see and feel her heart breaking. She was my very best friend in the entire world—the epitome of loyalty. If Lou was interested in someone else, Ter would be devastated.

I sat on the front stoop of our house the next morning waiting for Ter to pick me up for school. Another sleepless night had left me exhausted and pale. I'd tried to camouflage my appearance with extra blusher and even lipstick. And I was trying my best not to eat it off.

I stared down the driveway. My mother had the gardener plant masses of pink begonias and geraniums all along the drive up to the house. The wind made them toss their rosy heads. It was a defiant gesture, as if to say, "Nothing will crush us, not even the wind." I wished I could feel the same way. But I did feel crushed, pressed flat, weighted down.

Ter roared up the street and slammed to a stop at the curb. I rose, forcing a smile on my face, and joined her in the car.

"Sorry I'm late," Ter said breathlessly. "I couldn't figure out what to wear this morning." She didn't look at me. I knew she needed to concentrate on the road, but still, a glance before putting the car in gear would have been normal behavior for her.

She suspects, I thought in horror. No. That was ridiculous. How could she possibly know? I told myself.

We drove to school in silence, with me hanging on for dear life. Ter was driving as if she were in the Indianapolis 500. We roared into the parking lot and jumped out as the tardy bell went off.

135

"The only good thing about today is that we get to practice after school before you go to work," Ter said as we pounded down the quad toward our classrooms. "I have a great idea for a name for our band."

"What is it?" I asked with interest.

"Tell you later," she said, and sprinted off to her homeroom.

ten

At the end of the day, Ter and I met Scott outside
the band room before orchestra.

"Hey! We've got a gig!" he announced jubilantly.

"What? I can't believe it!" Ter cried. "We
haven't even come up with a name yet. How did
anyone hear of us?"

Scott beamed. "Well, my dad was talking to
one of his customers. And he told him about
the band we were forming. . . ."

"Yeah, and so?" I asked in excitement.

"Shh. Let him finish," Ter said, holding a finger
up to her mouth.

"So the guy owns a coffeehouse near the
beach in Avila, and he has two bands play there

every Friday and Saturday night." Scott's eyes gleamed as he spoke. "Anyway, there's going to be a spot open in a couple of weeks because of some kind of scheduling glitch. The band that was supposed to open for the Regents had to cancel out or something. So . . ." Scott said, taking a deep breath, "he asked my dad to see if we wanted to fill in!"

Ter and I looked at each other and gasped.

Scott raised his hands for us to keep quiet. "Of course, he wants to come over to Lou's to hear us first," he added. "But if we aren't half bad, we're in!"

Ter and I hugged each other, jumping up and down.

"Do you think we're good enough?" I asked.

"I hope so," Scott said seriously. "But he's not coming to hear us play until next Saturday, so we have to practice as much as possible this week."

"Has Lou heard yet?" Ter asked, glancing around.

"Yeah, he's inside tightening his drums," Scott said, nodding vigorously. He had a huge grin on his face.

I was grinning too, but though I knew a gig was ultimately what we'd hoped for, I was scared. Would any of us get stage fright? Would we blow our chance from nerves?

Mr. Marsh's voice rang out from inside the

band room, and the three of us hustled inside and took our places. I refrained from looking up at the drum section, but I wondered why Lou hadn't been there when Scott told us the good news. Had he been avoiding me? Or was I reading too much into his actions?

After school, Scott grabbed my hand. "Come on, Krista," he said. "Lou can ride with Teresa." Before I could answer, he had already pulled me out of the room.

The four of us descended on Lou's house, and bustled into the garage. We were all on such a high that we looked as if we were on a VCR tape on fast forward. In record time we had our instruments set up. Then we gathered around and tried to figure out what to play for our audition. As I called out my suggestions, I suddenly remembered that Ter had thought of a name for our group.

"Ter, tell us the name you thought up," I said.

The guys looked at her. "You got one?" Scott asked.

"Well, I don't know how good it is," Ter said, looking a little nervous.

"Come on. Just tell us," Scott urged. "It's gotta be better than nothing."

Ter took a deep breath. "High Pressure," she said, her expression even more tension filled than before.

We stared at her without saying anything. Then Lou said, "High Pressure?"

"Yeah. You see, I was trying to come up with a name using my feelings," Ter explained. "And I thought about how playing in the band had brought some excitement into my life. So I thought, maybe we can call ourselves Excitement. Then I decided to look up the word in the thesaurus, and that's where I found High Pressure."

Scott repeated the name a couple of times, and each time he said it with more enthusiasm. "You know? I like it," he said finally. Then he looked at me and Lou. "What do you think?"

"Sounds fine, amigo," Lou agreed.

"I think it's great," I said, smiling at Ter. I knew she needed to have her idea accepted enthusiastically, or she'd think everyone was just acquiescing out of a lack of a better choice.

"High Pressure it is, then," Scott said. "Now we just have to come up with some music."

"I think we ought to play Lou's piece," Ter suggested.

Lou started to object, but Scott overruled him. "Yeah, definitely. And we also need something more recognizable," he said. "We can do the familiar songs first and maybe close with Lou's piece. So what do you guys think."

"Great," I put in. "And we should do *Tell It Like*

140

It Is first. If our name is High Pressure, we need a rocker to open with."

"Right," Scott said, taking up his electric guitar. "Why don't we try that song now?"

The rest of us grabbed up our instruments and waited for Lou to give us our cue. He counted out three beats with his sticks, nodded, and we went right into it.

I was playing pretty well, and I was amazed that I managed to submerge myself in the music so that I hardly even noticed Lou. He was set up behind Scott and me, and I couldn't see him from where I stood, and it helped. If I had had to look at him, I don't think I could have kept my concentration.

After practice, we filed into Lou's house for snacks. The guys wolfed down chips and salsa, and Ter took a piece of paper and tried to work out a new practice schedule. I just stared at my hands, which were wrapped around a can of soda, in an effort to avoid making eye contact with Lou. Ter's voice washed over me as she went over everyone's work hours. I wanted to get out of there—out of Lou's kitchen and away from him. My efforts to not look at him were really beginning to wear me down.

"Okay, listen up, everyone. This is it," Ter announced, waving the schedule in the air. "Tomorrow's out. Krista and I work Wednesdays.

But we have Thursday, all afternoon and evening. We'll have to just stay here and practice like crazy from right after school until we collapse. Friday, Krista and I work, so that's out. But we've got Saturday morning and afternoon, since Scott doesn't work then." She looked at each of us, her eyes round and alert. "Do you realize how little time we have to prepare for this guy who's going to hear us?" she said.

Scott and Lou nodded, and I gave a ragged sigh. "I hope we're ready come Saturday," I said.

"We just have to be," Scott stated emphatically.

Ter took me home, talking nonstop about how incredible it was that we were going to have a chance to play for an audience. I was pretty excited too, but I also wished that Scott had arranged for us to practice in front of some of our friends. That way we'd know how we sounded to someone other than ourselves. And maybe we'd have more confidence about playing in front of a paying audience.

Then Ter started to talk about Lou again, which made me tune out and stare glassy eyed out the window. It occurred to me then that Thursday night was going to be tough. I would have to remain in the same room with Lou for roughly six hours straight.

When I got home I marched directly to my room and took out a large photo of Ter. I placed it on my music stand as if erecting a shrine. And in a sense it was a shrine. It was a tribute to so many years of a great friendship with a truly wonderful friend. I would never jeopardize my friendship with Ter. I would *never* go after a guy she was seeing. Of course, if it worked out the other way . . . if Lou were to show interest in me . . . A little spark of hope flared briefly in my heart, like a match, but before I could carry the thought too far, I snuffed it out. No. Even if Lou made the first move, it would still be an act of betrayal.

I called my mother before leaving work the next night to see if she needed anything. For all her organization, she gets a little out of whack when it comes to keeping the kitchen stocked. So I'd gotten into the habit of checking in with her before coming home. And sure enough, she needed orange juice.

I drove south on the highway, telling myself that it would be silly to go to a large grocery store for one item. A small store—like the Quick Stop—would make a lot more sense. But to go there would really be pushing my luck. It would be like reaching out to touch fire knowing full well you're going to get burned.

Somehow the fear of being burned wasn't a big enough deterrent. Or maybe, on a subconscious level, I wanted to get burned. I exited the highway and parked in front of Lou's father's store. Maybe Lou wasn't working tonight anyway, I told myself, but I knew full well he probably was.

When I stepped through the door and saw him, I felt like bubbles were traveling up my body and popping in my head. He was wiping down the glass doors of the freezer section. I slowly made my way over to the refrigerator section and began searching for the orange juice.

"Krista," he said from right beside me.

I turned to him and smiled. "Hi. My mother needed orange juice," I explained unnecessarily.

He nodded. "Oh." He was looking at me intently.

I felt as if I were on fire. Blindly, I reached for a quart of juice and clutched it to my chest. The shock of the cold container woke me up and, with a start, I edged toward the front of the store.

Lou followed after me.

"Scott was just here," he reported. "You just missed him."

"Oh" was all I could think of to say.

Lou stepped behind the register and rang up my juice. "That's $2.95," he said.

"Okay." I took out three singles and handed them to him.

He took them from my hand slowly "He was talking about you," he said tentatively.

"Oh really?" I answered inadequately. I wondered if he was expecting me to react in a particular way.

"Yeah. He's always talking about you," he said.

I didn't say anything. Why was he telling me this? I wondered.

"You nervous?" he asked as he gave me my change.

"W-what?"

"About Saturday."

"Oh." I gave a kind of strangled laugh. He'd changed the subject on me, I realized. "Yeah," I answered. "You?"

"Sure. I just hope we don't blow it." His eyes stared into mine. Was he talking only about music? Or was there more meaning in what he was saying?

"That would be terrible," I said, still looking at him.

"Yeah."

He handed me the orange juice in a paper bag. I took it, my eyes focusing on his hands. He had long fingers—musician's hands. They were the color of caramel. Beautiful hands for a guy. I ripped my gaze from them and looked up at him. He had a funny-looking smile on, kind of a lopsided slant on his mouth. His lips . . . how would it feel to . . . ? I trampled down the rest of that thought.

"Well, see you tomorrow," I said, backing away from the counter.

"Yeah." His dark eyes lingered on my face. I was having trouble breathing.

I somehow managed to get out the door and back to my car, moving like a sleepwalker. Dropping behind the wheel, I let myself look into the store one more time and was just in time to see Lou slam his fist into the metal frame of the freezer door. My God! I thought in shock. Why did he do that?

Once I got home, I put the orange juice away and went to my room. I lay down on my bed without turning on the lights and closed my eyes. Had it been my imagination that Lou's eyes had said things his mouth didn't? Was it just wishful thinking on my part to imagine that he might actually be attracted to me?

I thought about how he'd hit the freezer door. If he *did* like me, I reasoned, he'd be facing the same struggles I was experiencing. Like me, Lou would be trapped by his loyalty to Scott and unable to betray his friend, even if it meant denying himself something he wanted.

I flicked on the bedside lamp, and my glance fell on a photo album beneath it. I sat up, pulling the album into my lap. I opened to the first page. It was like reading an autobiography. My childhood lay before me. I had written all kinds of silly captions under the pictures. There was a snapshot of the time Ter and I had wanted to go camping in our backyard. We were eight, and my father had erected a tent for us. We had been afraid of the dark, so he had pulled out an extension cord and plugged in my Mickey Mouse night-light. "The brave explorers," I'd written underneath the photo. I laughed. It was all so silly.

Then there was a picture of Ter and me playing in a recital, a picture of us dressed for our first date back in ninth grade, a picture of Cathy and Jojo, Ter and me lying in our bathing suits on the patio with our noses covered in zinc ointment. "Sex goddesses at play," the caption read.

I pried open the plastic sheet over a letter Ter had sent me after I had moved to Washington. She'd written that she missed me. Cathy and Jojo were nice, she'd said, but nothing was the same without me. I remembered how I had felt the day I got that letter. . . .

And suddenly all my emotions welled up inside me. "Oh, Ter," I said out loud. A hot wet tear rolled down my cheek, falling on the letter and staining it. "I can't do this to you!"

"You guys want to try that again?" Scott asked, running a chord up and down his guitar.

"Yeah, okay," Lou mumbled.

Teresa shrugged. "Fine with me," she said. "We weren't exactly sensational."

"Krista?"

Scott's voice startled me to attention. "Um, yeah," I replied.

Scott looked at me for a second, then shook his head. "Okay, from the top," he called out.

We broke into the first bars of Heart's *Tell It Like It Is,* but I couldn't seem to get into the music. There was so much tension between Lou and me now, yet we both acted as if nothing was unusual. My head felt as if it were filled with scrambled eggs. Then my fingers stumbled over a note that sounded obscene, making the others stop playing instantly.

"Whoops," Scott said, touching my shoulder. "You got a sour note there." He looked at me with concern.

"Sorry," I said, looking down quickly.

"Hmm," Scott said thoughtfully. "Maybe I shouldn't have told you guys about Saturday."

When we'd met outside the band room before orchestra that day, Scott had had more great news. The man who owned the coffeehouse was going to give us a chance to play for an audience that same Saturday of our audition. He told Scott he'd listen to us in the morning, and that if we were good enough, we could play that night.

So today's practice was even more important now. It was our last rehearsal before Saturday.

And I was playing as if I had palsy.

"Count of three, guys," Scott instructed.

Lou did the count, and the rest of us joined in. But within sixty seconds, it became apparent that I wasn't the only one having trouble. Scott signaled for us to stop. Then he turned around and looked at Lou.

"Amigo, it might be my imagination, but your drums sound like they've got a terminal disease," he said lightly. "Can you give them resuscitation so they'll keep up?"

Scott was clearly joking, but Lou didn't look amused. "Yeah," he said tersely.

Raising one eyebrow in consternation, Scott said, "I think we're just a little bit overplayed right now. We've been at this for three hours anyway. Why don't we just can this tonight?"

Lou was watching him without emotion.

Scott went on. "We're probably all crazy thinking about Saturday morning," he said. "Maybe we'd better just chill out for the rest of the night. What do you think?"

Scott was being incredibly nice, I thought. It was only me and Lou who were playing badly, yet Scott wasn't pointing any fingers at us. I sort of wished he'd been disgusted with us. If he'd yelled at us, it would have eased some of the guilty feelings that swamped me.

"Well, since nobody's arguing, I guess that means yes," Scott said. "So let's go have a few snacks." He looked at Lou. "Where's the stuff, amigo?"

Lou didn't answer right away. "There's some chips and soda in the house," he said, fiddling with his drumsticks.

"Chips and soda?" Scott repeated incredulously. "No chili con queso?"

"I wasn't in the mood to cook last night," Lou said dully.

Scott walked over to Lou and felt his forehead. "Nope. There's no fever," he teased. "But you must be sick. That explains why you don't seem to know which end of the drumstick to use tonight."

Lou gave a half smile, then I suddenly realized that his eyes were fixed on me. Don't, I begged. Don't stare at me that way. Something in his expression had made weird little shivers run races up my spine.

He looked away quickly, as if I'd spoken out

loud, and for one terrified moment I wondered if I had.

"Ter," I said after a moment. "I'm not feeling so great. I—I have a headache." It was a white lie. A part of me did ache, but it wasn't my head. I looked at Ter pleadingly. "Can we go home now?"

"Oh, Krista, can't you take some aspirin?" Ter asked, obviously not ready to leave yet. She looked as if she were ready to send down roots right next to Lou, and I felt like a world-class creep.

"I don't think there's enough aspirin in the whole town to take care of this headache," I answered, fumbling with my guitar strap.

"Well, okay," Ter said reluctantly. She walked over to Lou and put her arms around his neck. "I hope you feel better soon, too," she said in a voice just barely loud enough for me to hear. She planted a big kiss on his mouth before turning to leave.

I put down Scott's guitar, hoping no one would notice my jerky, uncoordinated movements.

Scott walked me over to Ter's car and took me into his arms. He kissed me slowly and for a long time. "We'll do okay, Krista, on Saturday. Believe it," he whispered.

I wished I could.

eleven

By ten o'clock Saturday morning, the four of us were gathered in Lou's garage, practicing while we waited for the owner of the coffeehouse. Each of us was reacting to the pressure in different ways. Scott was the most confident, but also the most frenetic. He seemed to be jumping instead of walking, and he danced around while he played his guitar.

Ter seemed a little subdued. But I knew that was a cover up for a severe case of nerves. Her face was serious and expressionless, and on the keyboard her manner was studious—almost like a classical concert pianist's.

Lou appeared to be completely focused on his drums. He never looked up from them, which

152

was unusual because he could play those drums like John Bonham without ever looking at them.

And I felt as if I were playing under the influence of a really strong cold remedy, the kind that makes you feel like all your limbs are weighted with five-pound sacks of flour. My brain sent messages to my hands, but my hands weren't getting them fast enough.

Despite our agitated states, Scott seemed happy with our playing. He told us we were terrific and wonderful, and he had us so pumped up by the time we did our audition that I think we all believed in our imminent success.

Ed Kingston, the owner of the coffeehouse, came in wearing scruffy blue jeans, a sport shirt, and sneakers. He didn't exactly fit my idea of what the owner of a popular night spot would look like. He introduced himself to each of us, then said, "Okay, let's see what you've got." He stepped back, taking up a position far away from the amplifiers, then nodded for us to begin.

We played the first number pretty well, then got better with the second, and by the time we'd moved on to the piece Lou wrote, it was as if Ed Kingston were invisible. We really got into it, and while each of us played our solos, the others smiled encouragingly.

The last notes sounded, and Mr. Kingston immediately broke into applause.

"Tonight," he said. "The show begins at eight thirty." He smiled at us approvingly. "Come around seven thirty to set up." He shook hands with each of us, then gave Scott directions to his place and left.

We stared at each other in shock.

"That's it?" Ter said in disbelief. "Just like that? We're in?"

Scott whooped and ran a wild series of notes up and down his electric guitar. Ter and I hugged each other. And Lou pounded on his drums, bouncing his sticks off the heads and into the air, then catching them to bang out more rhythms.

Scott put his guitar down and came over to pick me up off my feet. As my legs dangled in midair, he danced around in circles. Ter pranced over to Lou, and the two of them hugged. Then they kissed—and I closed my eyes to blot out the sight of it.

I felt my feet hit the garage floor as Scott put me down. He whooped again and ran over to pound his best friend on the back. Lou punched him in the arm in return. Affection, male style, I thought, smiling at Ter.

"Okay," Scott said, finally getting himself calmed down enough to speak. He rubbed his hands together excitedly. "Lou and I will come to your house, Krista, at seven. And you two can follow us in Ter's car." He stopped speaking as if an idea had suddenly come to him. "You know, soon we're going to need some kind of transportation that can carry all four of us and our instruments," he said.

"Amigo," Lou said with a smile. "This is only our *first* gig. We may not get any more after tonight." He laughed. "So get a grip, okay?"

We were all behaving as though someone had just pumped laughing gas into the garage. But Lou was right. We really shouldn't get ahead of ourselves, I thought. We'd just had a good audition in front of one man, but that didn't mean we'd do as well in a coffeehouse full of strangers.

That night something happened just before the show that really affected my performance. We had been setting up our instruments, and Ter and I were helping Lou haul his drums out on the small stage. Scott was setting up an amplifier and needed help plugging it in. He turned toward Ter and me. "Hey, can one of you give me hand?" he asked.

Ter had been holding a drum, so she set it on the ground and clapped the dust off her hands. "Why?" she asked brightly. "Want to get used to hearing applause?"

I giggled.

"Funny girl," Scott said, faking a fierce expression. "As long as you have free hands, come over here and plug this amp in."

Ter trotted over, grinning unabashedly.

I continued to help Lou with his equipment, though I was feeling a little edgy. He reached for the cymbals I was handing to him, and I think I must have let go too soon. Lou lunged for the cymbals. I lurched forward, trying to retain my hold on the metal disks. We collided, Lou's hands suddenly making contact with my body. One of the cymbals clanged noisily to the ground.

Then Lou's arms were wrapped around me, the other cymbal wedged between us. Our faces were within inches of each other. I could hear his breathing. My skin seemed on fire where his arms touched me. I pulled back, the cymbal falling out of my grip. But Lou caught it before it hit the floor.

My face was flaming. "I'm so sorry!" I said in a scratchy and weak voice.

"It's okay," he said softly, looking at me with kind, gentle eyes.

Right then Mr. Kingston pushed through the drapes at the side of the stage. "Five minutes, kids," he said.

Scott yelped. "Let's hustle."

In four minutes and thirty seconds, we had the

rest of the instruments set up and were standing at our places, ready to be introduced. The small drapes parted, and suddenly there we were, on stage. Scott nodded, and Lou began his count. I played fine until right before we went into Lou's piece. Scott had mentioned to the audience that our last song would be a piece written by our drummer. He had nodded in Lou's direction, and I'd turned around.

Lou's eyes had met mine in that instant, and a funny little smile played across his mouth. He likes me, I suddenly realized. I could see it in his expression so clearly. I stared at him hard for a second and saw in his eyes the emotion I both wanted and feared. He was attracted to me!

I was filled with wonder. Elation that he felt the same way I did flooded through my body, making me feel like shouting for joy.

Then I came crashing down. Ter, whom I love more than a sister, was crazy about him. What was I going to do?

Wrestling with my emotions made me blow a few notes in my solo, and Lou, whose solo was right after mine, seemed to have caught bad vibes from me. His drum solo wasn't nearly as spectacular as it normally was. We finished the piece in a kind of pitiful slump, Lou's and my weak performances infecting Ter and Scott.

The curtain slowly closed as the audience

applauded. Then we all looked at each other, partly in relief and partly in disappointment.

Scott spoke first. "Man, I guess our nerves were shot by the time we got to Lou's piece, huh?"

I blinked and stared at him. I felt as if I were melting into a puddle.

"You all right, Krista?" I heard Ter ask me. Her voice seemed so far away, but she was actually right next to me.

I turned toward her and her face slowly came into focus.

"Uh, yeah," I managed to get out. "I'm so sorry. I was doing okay until—" My voice trailed off. What could I possibly say?

"Yeah," she said, her face creased with concern.

"Amigo," Scott said to Lou. "You surprised me. I thought you were the coolest one of us all. You kinda lost it on your drum solo, huh?"

Lou looked down at the floor without reacting.

"I guess we can chalk this up to being whacked out by our first gig," Scott said. "I mean, probably all bands get crazy the first time they play before an audience."

"That's right," Ed Kingston said, coming onto the stage. Incredibly he was smiling. "You kids did okay. Not great, but okay," he said unenthusiastically. "If you want to, you can still play that spot in three weeks."

We stared at him in disbelief.

"Really?" Scott said.

"Really," Mr. Kingston said. "Now get your stuff off the stage. The Regents need it." He turned abruptly and left us to remove our equipment.

We collected our instruments as quickly as possible and hustled out to our cars. Then Mr. Kingston came out to hand Scott our check. "See you in three weeks," he said. "Eight thirty."

We watched him go back into the coffeehouse. Then Scott turned toward us, waving the check in the air. "I told you we could do it!" he yelled happily. "Our first two hundred dollars!"

We crowded around, taking turns holding the check in our hands. "Next time we'll be used to the stage thing," Scott predicted. "And we'll be better."

I looked at Scott and had to smile. He was so encouraging—so *nice*. And at that moment he was beaming, obviously filled with so much happiness. *Oh, Scott,* I thought. *Why can't you be the one I want?* It didn't seem fair. He was wonderful in so many ways, but I just couldn't like him in the same way he liked me.

I needed space to think. I needed to go home. But Scott wanted us to go out and celebrate.

So I lied. I pleaded a headache. I begged Ter

159

to take me home and I told the rest of them to go out without me. I apologized for being a wet blanket, but I really, really didn't feel well, I told them. Ter and Scott tried to change my mind, but I refused and won. Ter took me home.

"I hope you feel better," Ter said, delivering me to my door. A worried frown creased her face. "Maybe you ought to go to a doctor," she added. "I mean, this is the second time you've had a headache so bad you had to be taken home."

"Oh, Ter, you always make things out to be bigger than they are," I said. "A good night's sleep will take care of this."

"Well, okay," Ter said. "See you tomorrow?"

"Yeah."

I entered my house, hearing the buzz of the television in the family room. And I could hear my mother's voice talking to someone on the phone in the kitchen. I was thankful my parents were distracted. That way I could make it to my room without being apprehended and subjected to the third degree. I knew they'd want to know how our first gig went.

I walked as silently as fog down the carpeted hallway and entered my room, closing the door softly behind me. I found my way over to my window in the dark by memory and stared out at the street. Ter's car was gone, but the words she spoke in the car on the way over were still ringing in my ears.

"Don't you think Lou is just wonderful?" Ter had said. "It was obvious his nerves weren't the best tonight, but he tried to play that drum solo as well as he could. . . . He looked so handsome sitting there behind those drums. . . . I'll bet so many girls sitting in the audience were panting after him. . . . I can't believe I've got a guy as fabulous as he is interested in me. . . . This is it, Krista! It has to be."

Ter's words were clear in my memory. She had been exuberant tonight, but I thought I detected a desperate ring in her voice. It was almost as if she were trying to convince us both that what she was saying was true.

"Oh, Krista, can't you just feel it? You and Scott, me and Lou. We're the couples of the year. Even the way we look together is perfect. You and Scott are both tall and blond. Lou and I are darker and more compact."

Not that much more compact, my traitorous mind had argued. Lou still had two inches on me. But in a way, I wished he was ten inches shorter than me. Maybe then I wouldn't be attracted to him.

Ter had kept up a steady commentary on Lou's attributes all the way to my house. I had worked so hard to keep from screaming at her to be

161

quiet that by the time I'd gotten home, I was wiped out.

But Ter was right, I thought, standing by the window. Lou was wonderful—he was kind, hard working, good looking, and he really listened when someone talked to him. Of course, it occurred to me that that description could also apply to Scott. But I still couldn't work up the feelings for Scott that I had for Lou.

I tore myself away from the window and snapped on my dresser lamp. The first thing I saw was the photograph of Ter I'd put on the music stand. There was a sheet of music sticking up behind it, so I walked over and pulled it out. It was the last piece Ter and I had practiced before school started. Before the band got together, Ter and I used to practice violin together at my house. We'd been doing that since seventh grade, and my father had even bought Ter a music stand of her own to place next to mine in my room. My eyes traveled to the spot where her stand used to be, and a tear rolled down my cheek. So many memories.

I started peeling off my clothes. The memories of the past were bright and un-complicated. But now it seemed that nothing was carefree and easy, and my life was like a dark puzzle I couldn't solve.

The phone beside my bed rang the next morning, waking me from a long and heavy sleep. It was Ter. She wanted to come over, but I told her I had to do research at the library for my economics report.

"Is there something wrong, Krista?" she asked, sounding hurt and confused. "Did I do something to make you mad?"

"Ter, no. Why would you think that?"

"It's just that you've seemed kind of funny lately. I can't figure out what it is exactly but—"

"Ter, there's nothing wrong. Really," I insisted. "I just have that rotten report for Hernandez hanging over my head, and I really have to start working on it." I paused, waiting for a response, but she remained silent. "Believe me, Ter. That's all it is," I said. But although I did have a report to work on, I was really going to the library to get away from everyone. I needed the time to be by myself, away from anything and anyone that might remind me of my problem.

"Well, okay," she said dubiously.

I stared at the phone after we hung up, hating the way I felt—disloyal and even dishonest. I didn't want to lie to my best friend, but I told myself that it was necessary. I had too many issues to work out within myself before I could handle spending time with Ter again.

I had my mother drop me off at the library as soon as it opened that afternoon.

"Call me when you need a ride home," she said as I stepped out of the car.

I nodded, then walked up the stairs and entered the building. Briefly I entertained hopes that Lou would be there, too, but then I remembered he'd photocopied a lot of material the last time I saw him in the library, so he probably wouldn't need to come back. I knew seeing him again would only fuel my attraction toward him and confuse me even more, but I couldn't help wishing that I'd run into him again.

I placed my notebook and economics text down on a table, then headed for the aisle where I knew the economics books were shelved. I whipped around the end of one aisle and crashed right into someone walking in the opposite direction.

"Oof!" I exclaimed, bouncing backward and stumbling into the shelves behind me. I grabbed onto some books to keep myself from wiping out on the floor, then realized it was Lou who had collided into me.

"Krista!" he said, stepping back.

We stared at each other, neither of us moving. My breath was tight in my chest, as if my lungs had suddenly shrunk in half. I felt myself moving slowly toward him, and the distance between us was shrinking bit by bit. Then his face was so close to mine that I could practically feel his breath against my skin. Our lips met, and I felt his hand press gently on my back. I opened my eyes halfway, but shut them again when Lou pulled me flat against him. We kissed again and again. They were quick, urgent kisses, as if they were the first kisses either of us had ever experienced.

But then a voice washed over us like icy water. "Disgusting! In a library!"

We jerked away from each other and saw an older woman push past us scowling and muttering under her breath. She paused at the end of the aisle and glared at us before reaching for a book.

Without warning, Lou grabbed my hand and pulled me after him. I stumbled behind him, wondering where he was taking me. He passed a table, pausing only long enough to grab up some books with his free hand. Then he began scanning the room, and I realized that he was looking for my stuff. I led him to the table where I had set down my books, and he swiped them up before I even had a chance to touch them. Then he hauled me toward a side exit, and we burst out into the parking lot.

His truck was parked nearby. He opened the door, and I climbed in. I knew I was acting on impulse, but his kisses had left my mind in such a muddled state that I couldn't think straight.

He got in on the other side of the truck and threw our things in the backseat. Then he slid in close to me and wrapped me tightly in his arms. He kissed me slowly, and this time no one stopped us.

When we finally pulled away from each other, my breath came out jagged and shallow. Lou kept one arm wrapped around my waist, holding me so tightly that it almost hurt.

"I've been wanting to do that for days," he said, letting out a long breath.

I looked at him and smiled.

"But, uh, I've got something I want to say." He shifted his eyes away from me nervously. "I know Scott's crazy about you," he went on. "And it's no secret Teresa likes me a lot more than I like her."

I winced at his words. I was guilty of betraying Ter, but another part of me was still looking out for her. And in spite of myself, I hated to hear that Lou didn't feel the same affection for her as she did for him.

Lou went on. "That first day in orchestra, Scott noticed you immediately. He made it clear that he was interested in you, and he tried to convince me that Teresa and I looked perfect for each other." He paused as if he were gathering his thoughts. "Anyway, it didn't matter to me. I didn't know who you were, so I was open to the idea of dating Teresa." He swallowed before going on. "But then I got to know you and found out I really like you—more than Teresa. She's pretty and nice, but I'm just not attracted to her. I feel bad about that, but—" He took a deep breath. "But I want to go out with *you*." He looked directly into my eyes. "So, uh, how do you feel about that?"

I was so thrilled that I wanted to shout. But when I spoke, my voice sounded small and meek. "I want to go out with you, too," I said.

"Great," he said, smiling. Then he cradled my face in his hands and kissed me.

twelve

"So what are we going to do about Scott and Teresa?" Lou asked after our long deep kiss.

"Oh, I don't want to hurt her," I said, dropping my face into my hands. "She's my best friend." I sat up in my seat and let my hands fall into my lap. "Ter's crazy about you," I said. "She's so sure you guys are perfect for each other. I know she'd be so hurt if she ever found out about—about us."

Lou squeezed his eyes shut and let his head fall back against the headrest. I knew he didn't like what he was hearing, but I had to go on.

"I've never done anything to hurt Ter," I said in a barely audible voice. "And I don't want to do it now."

"I hear you," Lou said, taking my hand. "I feel the same way about Scott. We've been buddies so long it's like he's a member of my family."

I nodded.

"And I know how he feels about you. He's told me often enough." Lou paused for a moment and stared out through the windshield. "Scott's liked girls before," he went on, "but this time he says it's different. None of the other girls shared his interest in music like you do."

He rubbed a hand over his eyes as if they hurt. When he started speaking again, his voice sounded thick and sluggish. "I don't want to hurt Scott either, and if he finds out about us, I know he won't want to have anything to do with us ever again."

My body started to tremble. Lou put his arms around me and hugged me close. Then I began to cry.

"Krista, don't," Lou said gently. He kissed me until the trembling stopped, but tears were streaming down my cheeks.

"Oh, I don't know what to do," I said miserably. "I want to be with you, but I don't want to destroy the best friendship I'll ever have."

"I know," he said, wiping my cheeks dry.

We sat in silence for a while, just holding each other. I could hear the distant sounds of people laughing, car doors opening and closing, and engines starting. But the world outside seemed remote to me.

Finally Lou spoke up. "I think this is what we should do," he began. "Since neither of us wants to hurt Scott or Ter, and since we haven't had the chance to really get to know each other, why don't we go out a few times without telling anyone?" He looked at me out of the corner of his eye.

It sounded to me like he was proposing something underhanded. "You mean secretly date each other?" I asked, holding my breath.

"Yeah," he said, sighing. "It'll be hard not to get, uh, found out, but what if we discover later on that we really aren't that nuts about each other? Then we would have hurt them for nothing."

I considered his point. "I don't know . . ." I said, shaking my head.

"Listen, Krista," he said, speaking slowly. "It wouldn't make any sense to break up with them until we're absolutely sure about *us*."

"But I—I don't think I can do that," I said hesitantly. "It seems so sneaky."

Lou sighed. "I know. You're right. It is sneaky. So maybe we should just forget about the whole thing, huh?"

I looked into his eyes. They were warm and

dark and full of emotion. I wanted him. But I didn't want to hurt Ter or Scott. Lou did have a point, though. We might find out that we didn't like each other as much as we thought, and maybe things wouldn't work out between us. "I guess we should give it a try," I said, feeling relieved that we had come to a decision, but terrified that we might get caught and end up hurting two people we cared about.

Lou pulled me tightly against his chest. I could hear the heavy beat of his heart and the sound of his breathing. "Then that's what we'll do," he said with finality.

I buried my face deeper into his chest. I didn't want to go through with it, but I saw no other way.

"Teresa and Scott work Mondays," he said tentatively. "But we don't. So do you want to do something tomorrow night?"

I lifted my face and nodded.

"Okay then. It's set," he said. Then his smile faded suddenly. "I guess I can't really pick you up at home without your parents knowing, can I?" he said.

I thought about my parents' schedules for a second. "Actually," I said, "my mother has some meeting she has to go to tomorrow night, and Dad mentioned that he had an appointment, too. So I guess it'll be all right."

"Okay," he said. "So I'll come by and pick you up, and you can leave a note for your parents saying that a friend took you to the library or something."

"I guess that will work," I said. I wasn't really convinced that that would be a good enough excuse, but I didn't have a better idea.

"What time should I come around?" Lou asked.

"My parents should be gone by six thirty," I said.

"Okay," he said. "Well, I guess I'd better take you home now. It's getting late and don't you work now on Sundays?"

"Ugh, yes," I said with a glance at my watch. "In one hour."

Lou started his truck and headed for my house. But then he pulled over about a block before we got there and took me into his arms once again and kissed me.

I ran the rest of the way home and entered the house quietly. I was elated on the one hand, but I also felt trampled down by guilt. I knew no word strong enough to describe how Ter would feel if she found out about me and Lou. Guys had always taken advantage of Ter, and I had always been the one who helped her get over them. I had always looked out for her. And now, here I was, taking part in a plan that could hurt her more than all those guys combined.

It's kind of depressing to find out that you have

172

the capacity for deception. I never thought I had the skill to be sneaky. But I did. Monday morning I managed to act perfectly normal when Ter picked me up. Fortunately Ter was still excited about our successful gig at the coffeehouse, so I was able to steer the conver-sation in that direction, and I wasn't forced to talk about Lou.

But every period at school that day seemed to last as long as a year. I left each class not remembering anything the teacher had said. I couldn't even remember if they'd assigned any homework. All I could think about was my date with Lou, and I counted the minutes until six thirty.

Lou drove up to the curb outside my house right on time, and I sprinted out to his truck. I didn't want any of our nosy neighbors to see who was picking me up, in case any of them decided to say something to my parents.

"Hi!" I said, jumping into his truck with a huge grin on my face.

He gave me a warm, reassuring smile, then leaned over and pecked me on the cheek. As soon as he had put the truck into gear, he took my hand and held it. "I thought we could go see a movie," he said. "Is that all right with you?"

"Perfect," I said.

We chose a theater out of the way to lessen the chances of running into anyone we knew. It was also a school night, so we figured most of our friends would be staying home. I don't think either of us saw much of the movie, though. Throughout the film we just held each other and kissed. It was as if we both had an endless supply of pent-up emotion, accumulated over the past weeks.

We exited the mall and headed for Lou's truck. On the way home, I sat close to him and laid my head on his shoulder.

"Remember the last movie we saw?" I asked, lifting my head and looking at him.

He nodded. "Yeah. What about it?"

"Remember when your leg touched mine?"

He looked at me with a crooked smile on his face. "Yeah."

"Did you do that on purpose?"

He smiled.

"I thought so," I said, placing my head back on his shoulder.

"I wanted to touch you so badly," he explained, "and I couldn't think of any other way to do it."

We turned onto my street, and he parked a block away from my house as he had the night before. We huddled in the dark, talking.

"So your father owns that store you work in?" I asked.

Lou nodded.

"You look a little like him," I said, examining

his features. "But you look more like your mom."

"Yeah, that's what everyone says," he said. "She's only half Mexican, you know. The other half's Italian."

"Oh, really?"

He nodded.

"And you have a sister and two brothers, right?" I asked.

"Yep," he said. "And I'm the baby. My dad calls me the runt of his litter, and sometimes he just calls me Runt, like it's a name."

I laughed. "And you're taller than he is."

"I'm taller than all the rest of them, too," he said, laughing. Then suddenly he sobered.

"What is it?" I asked.

He answered abruptly. "Nothing."

I tried to read the expression on his face, but the darkness obscured his features, and he wouldn't meet my gaze. Then I remembered how his mood had changed the day we were having a picnic on the beach. Both Scott and Lou had clammed up at the mention of one of Lou's brothers—Roberto. I swallowed and placed a hand on his arm. "Lou," I said gently, "maybe it's none of my business, but what is it about your brother Roberto?"

"What do you mean?" he said defensively.

"I mean, your mood suddenly changed when

his name came up at the beach the other day," I said tentatively. "And now that we're talking about your family, something seems to be bothering you."

He looked out the window on his side, and I wondered if he was trying to hide his face from me. I reached out and touched his chin, turning his head back toward me. He looked at me with a haunted expression.

"Lou, it's all right," I said. "You don't have to—"

"Okay, here's the story," he said, cutting me off. His mouth was set in a tight line, and his voice sounded cold and distant. I tensed. "Roberto's the second child in my family. He's nineteen," he began evenly. "When he was fifteen, he got mixed up with the wrong crowd and started doing drugs. He eventually left home and moved to L.A. He started dealing there. Then he got caught—not just once, but three times. The last time he was carrying a knife and he injured an officer—"

I gasped. "No!"

"The cop almost died," he went on. "Anyway, now he's doing time."

I squeezed his hand. "I'm so sorry, Lou," I said. "Your parents must have been devastated."

Lou laughed bitterly. "Oh, yeah. My mother cried for weeks. And my dad . . ." He paused and took a deep breath. "He considers my

176

brother dead. The day they arrested him the last time, Dad went on a rampage in the room I shared with him, throwing everything that belonged to Roberto out in the trash. He even went through the photo albums and burned every picture he could find of Roberto."

I listened in horror as Lou continued speaking. Every word he uttered seemed to have been ripped from his throat.

"I thought he'd lost his mind," he said. "He could remove everything from our house that reminded us of Roberto, but didn't he understand that he could *never* remove him from our hearts?"

I heard his voice crack just before he spoke his last words. And I hugged him fiercely for a long time.

Then I felt his muscles begin to relax a bit, and I loosened my grip around him. "So that's the skeleton in my closet," he said in falsely hearty tone of voice.

"Why do you think your father reacted that way?" I asked.

Lou slouched down in his seat. "Because he used to live in a barrio in L.A., and he hated the way society never expected Chicanos to do well," he explained. "He moved the family up here when I was four, and he and my mother have struggled to make a good life for us."

I listened intently, trying to grasp what he was saying.

"All our lives he taught us how important it was to improve ourselves," Lou said. "He expected us to try as hard as we could in school. . . . I've always tried to live up to my father's expectations."

"And is that difficult?" I asked.

"Sometimes there's a lot of pressure," he replied. "My father always used to say, 'We Chicanos have to be better than everyone else just so they'll think we're half as good.' He told us that so often that we got sick of hearing it." He paused as if he were recalling a specific scene from years ago. "So after a while I just stopped listening. But Roberto started to become unglued. . . . I think he just rebelled too much. Anyway, what he did was a slap in the face to our father."

I remained silent, because I really didn't know what to say. Lou's life seemed so outside my realm of experience.

He squeezed me tightly against him. "Thanks for understanding about Roberto," he said. "Sometimes my other brother, Raul, and I go to visit him, but we don't tell Dad. He's not that far from here."

"Do you go often?" I asked.

"The last time I went was that Monday I came

by Taco Bell and found you working on your off night. Remember?"

"Yeah."

"And remember when you and Teresa came up to me after orchestra—the day Scott didn't show up in class?"

"Yeah," I said.

"Well, I went to see him that day too," he said. "In fact, I know I was acting funny that day— kind of distracted, and Ter was giving me confused looks." He laughed. "I always get uptight just before seeing Roberto. I'm sorry if I seemed rude."

"Does Ter know about this?"

"No. I don't talk about it much," he said. "I'm not exactly proud of what he did. But he's still my brother, and I . . . I love him."

We were silent for a while, but then I noticed the time on the lighted dial on the dashboard. It was almost ten thirty, and since the library closed at nine, I knew I'd have some heavy-duty excuse making to do at home.

"I better go," I said. "It's so late my parents are going to subject me to intense questioning."

Lou glanced at the clock. "Yeah, it *is* getting late," he said, opening the door on his side. He jumped out of the truck, came around to open my door, and lifted me down to the ground. Then he kissed me slowly, his fingers combing

179

through my long hair. Both my arms were wrapped around his neck, and I didn't want to let go. His lips were warmer and sweeter than I had ever experienced before. Finally, we parted.

"Good night, Krista," he whispered.

"Good night," I said. "And thanks."

He smiled and gave a small wave before getting back into his truck.

I ran toward the house and immediately saw that the lights in the living room were on and my father was sitting in his chair. Oh no, he's waiting, I thought. With my heart sinking into the pit of my stomach, I opened the door and went to face the jury.

"What I said was that I ran into a friend I hadn't talked to in a while, and we sat in her car and caught up on things." I had called Lou from the pay phone at work, and I was explaining to him what I'd said to my parents the night before. I'd found a note in my locker from Lou at school that day. *Call me from work tonight,* it read. *I'll be home. What happened with your folks?*

"Very skillful," he said in approval.

I laughed. "Thanks."

"It's going to be rough practicing Thursday night, you know," he said, switching gears on me.

"I know," I answered. "I just hope we can handle it."

Thursday night was worse than rough. It was torture. I was trying not to look at Lou, and I knew he was probably trying not to look at me. I wanted to throw myself into the music, but even that was difficult because we were practicing a new piece for the next gig and we were constantly stopping midway through the song. It was a duet, and somehow I had convinced Ter and Scott to try it together. "Just so we have some variety," I had said.

Ter's soprano voice seemed to complement Scott's baritone quite well. So when they finally got through the first take, I said, "You guys sound like your voices were made for each other." Even to my own ears, I sounded overly enthusiastic, and I realized that it was wishful thinking that had made me say that to them. I wanted *them* to be together instead of me and Scott. I wanted them to be a pair.

They looked at me and then each other, and shrugged. "We're not *that* good together," Scott said.

Ter turned to Lou. "Maybe we ought to try singing together," she suggested.

Oh, help, I thought when I saw him nod in

agreement. No. I can't stand to watch this.

But I did.

And I made it through the entire practice that night, through school the next day, and through Ter driving me to and from work Friday night. It cost me, though. When I went to bed on Friday night, I was so exhausted I felt as if I could sleep for a year.

Then just when I thought my endurance had been stretched to the limit, things got worse.

"I want to go out with just you, and not with Lou and Teresa," Scott said to me after a practice session Saturday morning.

I stared at him, speechless for an instant. "Uh . . . okay," I said lamely.

Scott frowned, looking at me as if I were a stranger. Then his mouth quirked. "How about tonight?" he asked. Kevin's having a party at his house. Want to go?"

Kevin Nakasawa was a pretty good friend of his, so I figured the party might be important to Scott. "Okay," I said, trying to infuse some enthusiasm into my voice.

"Pick you up at six then?" he said.

I nodded and smiled in spite of the fact that I really didn't feel like going.

Ter and Lou were working out a practice schedule for the next week. It was going to be very tricky. Lou had to work the nights Ter and I were free, so we were going to have to squeeze practice in between when school ended at three forty till one of us had to go to work at five. And my violin practice was really going to suffer. I hadn't had much time to practice violin in the past two weeks. Whenever I picked it up in orchestra, I wanted to strum it like a guitar. I knew I had to get with the program soon or else Mr. Marsh was going to regret his decision to let me into the class.

"It's so great that you and Scott are going out tonight," Ter said to me on the way home from Lou's. "I wish Lou didn't have to work or we could go out alone, too," she added wistfully. It took all my acting ability to give Ter the impression that I was sorry she couldn't be with Lou that night, but I think I managed to seem sincere.

And it took all my acting ability to pretend I was having fun with Scott that night. Kevin's house was packed with kids from school. They spilled out onto the patio, and a game of volleyball was in progress in his backyard. I followed Scott as he made his way through the house toward the patio where the food was set up. "Man, I'm famished. You hungry?"

"Sort of," I answered. I waved to Cathy, who was on the other side of the patio talking to

Kevin, and the two of them came toward us.

"Hi guys," Kevin said as he approached. "I hear you have a band going. What are the chances of hearing you play?"

I watched Scott closely. "Yeah, there are four of us in the band," he said blandly. "And, uh, there might be a chance to see us soon. I'll let you know."

My mouth dropped open. Why hadn't Scott mentioned the coffeehouse gig? I wondered. What was the big secret?

Kevin nodded. "Okay. Let me know," he said. "I'd love to see you." He went off to fill a plate with food, and Scott followed. I really didn't have much of an appetite, so I turned my attention to Cathy.

She was looking at me with shining blue eyes. "Every girl in school is so envious of you," she said. "So many girls would die to have Scott interested in them."

"Really?" I asked, surprised.

"Of course. He's a great catch." Cathy raised her eyebrows and grinned. "You're *so* lucky to have him. Of course, I happen to think he's pretty lucky to have you too." She leaned in closer. "People think you look great together."

"That's good, I suppose," I said, smiling in spite of the discomfort her remark had caused me. "Well, I guess I'd better go join him now," I said. Scott had taken his food over to the side of the patio, and he was signaling for me to come over.

I sat down next to him while he ate. "Why didn't you tell Kevin about the gig in Avila?" I asked in a low voice. "I thought he was a good friend of yours."

Scott frowned. "I want to make sure we play better than we did last time before we have kids from school see us." He must have caught the astounded look on my face, because he went on to explain. "I mean, we did have a few flubs, didn't we? I just think we should really get our act together before people we know hear us."

I wasn't sure I liked this perfectionist side of Scott. I thought having the kids hear us would make us do our best, but since Scott was the unofficial leader of the band, I decided to keep quiet.

For the rest of the evening, I sat on the patio with Scott, wishing I was someplace else. Part of me still tried to act like a perfect date. But another part counted the seconds until we could leave. And when Scott finally took me home and kissed me good night, it took everything I had to act as though I was enjoying it.

I stepped out of my clothes when I got up to my room, feeling totally worthless. I was completely shortchanging Scott, and he certainly didn't deserve it. But if I called it off with him, then I might cause the band to break up. I enjoyed playing in the band and I knew the other three loved it, too. I didn't want to be the person responsible for destroying a good thing.

thirteen

On Sunday afternoon Ter had to baby-sit her little brother. He was sick with the flu, running a temperature of 103, and there was no way she could leave him alone. When she told me this over the phone, I was relieved. Ter would be tied up for the day, and she couldn't even ask me to come over because I could catch the virus from Ricardo. So I was spared from coming up with an excuse for not spending time with her, and I was free to call up Lou to see if he wanted to do anything. As it turned out, Lou was free too, and he suggested that we drive over to Morro Bay.

The huge boulders at the base of Morro Rock have always been a favorite climbing place of mine, and I discovered that Lou loved it there, too. We held hands and clambered all over the giant rocks, laughing like little kids. Then we stood on the rocks by the ocean and watched monstrous waves crash below us. The white froth sprayed us, and sea gulls wheeled overhead, calling to each other.

After about an hour, we left the rocks and walked over to the beach. Some guys in wet suits were surfing in the waves, but otherwise no one else was around. We sat in the sand, holding hands and looking out at the bay and the ocean beyond. The surf pounded only thirty feet away, and fluffy white clouds scudded across the sky. I had never felt so alive. I had never felt so deliriously happy. I closed my eyes and willed time to stop so that the day would never end.

But soon we had to start heading back home so that I could go to work. We pulled ourselves away from the beach and climbed into Lou's truck. As we were tooling along the main street of Morro Bay, Lou suddenly yelped. "Get down quick! Scott's coming."

I didn't believe it at first, but then I recognized his Jeep approaching. I ducked out of view just barely before Lou said, "He's waving. I'll try to get by— Oh no! He's backing up. He's gonna think it's weird if I don't talk to him." The tone of his voice changed suddenly. "Hi, Scott! What are you doing up here?"

I could hear Scott's voice faintly. "Running an errand for Dad," he said. "What are *you* doing here?"

"Oh, you know. Just checking out the girls," Lou joked.

Scott chuckled. "Don't let Ter hear about this. She looks like the jealous type."

Lou laughed. "We'd better move, Amigo. We're blocking traffic."

"Yeah—see you later," Scott said. Then after a moment I heard the sound of an engine fade away in the distance.

Lou let out a long breath. "The coast is clear," he said.

I crawled back up to the seat. My legs had cramped up, and my nerves felt like over-tightened guitar strings.

I looked out the rear window and sighed. "I don't see how we can keep this up," I said. "What if we get caught the next time?"

Lou shrugged. "I don't know," he said, shaking his head.

For the rest of the drive home, Lou and I examined every single car we saw to see if it looked familiar. We hardly even talked because we were both too busy swivelling our heads every which way, peering into cars to see if we knew the driver. I was beginning to feel like an escaped convict on the run.

Once we got to our usual parking spot a block away from my house, we were both still shaken by the close call with Scott. With the tension between us so high, our kisses were hotter and more urgent than ever before. Lou held me so tightly, I couldn't breathe. We broke apart, gasping for air. After a moment, he leaned his forehead against mine and sighed. "What are we going to do, Krista?" he said desperately. "I want you, not Teresa. She's great, but she's just not for me."

"And I want to be with you," I whispered. "But if we tell Scott and Ter about us, they'll flip out."

"Or hate us forever," Lou said darkly.

He was right, I knew. Ter would never forgive me. And I didn't expect her to. When I thought about what my friendship with her meant to me, I was filled with dread. *Nothing*—maybe not even Lou—could ever replace the years I shared with Ter.

"Well," I said, breaking the silence. "I'm going to be late for work if I don't get going." I kissed Lou one more time and ran home.

For three weeks, I ached to be alone again with Lou. But because of our work schedules and the upcoming coffeehouse gig, we couldn't find the time to sneak away together. A couple of times I stopped by the Quick Stop when I knew Lou was working, and we had to content ourselves with just looking at each other. He stopped by Taco Bell one night, too, but the light chitchat that passed between us wasn't enough to satisfy my need to kiss him and be held by him.

The coffeehouse was packed the Saturday night of our show. We could feel the energy in the room as soon as the stage lights came on and we started playing. All four of us were perfectly in sync, and we gave a great performance.

As soon as the curtains closed over us, Mr. Kingston came to see us backstage. "There's a guy out front who wants to talk to you," he said. His face gave away nothing, and I couldn't tell if he was happy with our performance or disappointed.

The four of us exchanged puzzled looks. Then we cleared away our equipment from the stage and went to find the man Mr. Kingston had told us about.

As it turned out, the man who wanted to see us was the manager of a brand-new condominium complex. He pulled us aside at the back of the coffeehouse and bought us Cokes.

"We've built a complex for singles," he said.

"And we're looking for a band to play for a couple of hours at our open house for potential buyers."

I saw a grin spread across Scott's face.

"I like how you guys sound," the man went on. "And I like your name—High Pressure. Of course, you're a little younger than I had in mind, but I'm offering you the job anyway. We'll pay you two hundred dollars to play from two to five. Are you interested?"

Ter, Lou, and I all looked at Scott with wide eyes. He scanned our faces, then cocked his head in a gesture that seemed to say, "Should we do it?"

All three of us nodded.

"Okay," Scott said to the man.

The man shook hands with all of us. Then he gave us the address, and the four of us went backstage to take our instruments out to our cars.

"We're on our way!" Scott yelled, punching a fist into the air.

"We have to go celebrate this," Lou said. "Let's go have some Mexican food."

We chose a restaurant near the beach, and all the way there we repeated everything the manager had said over and over again. "I like how you guys sound." "You're a little younger than I had in mind. . . ." His words had meant everything to us, and we laughed as we relived the emotions we'd felt when he offered us the job.

The four of us squeezed into a booth at the restaurant. Ter was plastered against Lou's side, and Scott had his arm around me. It would have been easier for me if I hadn't had to sit directly across from Lou. It took so much effort not to look at him. I had to turn sideways, so that I was facing Scott and Ter more. But even then, I could still see Lou out of the corner of my eye.

Throughout the meal, Ter played with Lou's hand and gazed at him adoringly. I tried looking everywhere but at their entwined fingers, but somehow my eyes kept wandering back.

Then someone's foot nudged mine under the table, and I noticed Lou had a smirk on his face. He wasn't looking at me, but I knew it was his foot that had touched me. I was about to nudge him back playfully when he suddenly stomped on my toes. I jumped, and Lou put a hand over his mouth to hide his grin.

Scott frowned at me. "You sure are jumpy tonight, Krista. You're all over this booth. What's the matter?"

"Yeah," Ter said. "You're acting really strange. If I didn't know you any better, I'd think you were doing drugs."

I swallowed and grabbed my glass to take a sip.

My mouth had suddenly gone dry. "Of course I'm acting different," I said. "I'm part of a band that's being paid money to play." I looked at Ter as if she should have realized that. "It's pretty exciting, you know."

Ter nodded, but she still looked suspicious.

Scott squeezed me around the shoulders and grinned. "Well, get used to it," he said. "This is only the beginning."

His words echoed in my head. This is only the beginning. Scott looked into the future and saw the four of us together just the way we were. I assumed Ter did too.

I looked at Lou across the table from me. I wondered what he was thinking. *I* was thinking that he and I would have to be first-class creeps to crush the happiness Scott and Ter seemed to be feeling tonight.

Ter called after we'd both been taken home that night. I had already gone to bed, so I was surprised when the phone rang. "Krista, remember when I asked you to observe Lou and me when we're together?" she asked. "You know, to see if it looked like he liked me as much as I like him?"

"Yeah."

"Well, tonight I felt like . . . like he really *isn't* interested in me. I mean, he's nice to me. But he's always nice. I just don't think that he likes me the way I like him. So what do you think?"

I was thankful that Ter couldn't see my face, because I'm sure guilt was written all over it. I knew I had to choose my words with care.

"Ter, do you remember last year when you wrote me about how Jojo had a crush on Tim Spencer?"

"Yeah."

"And remember how you told her that maybe she just had to accept that things weren't going to click between them?"

"Yes, but I don't want it to be like that with Lou and me," Ter cried. "I want him to like me." Her voice was filled with grief, and I closed me eyes, trying to hold the tears in.

"Yeah, I know," I said in a soothing voice.

"Well, I'll just have to try harder to get him to like me," Ter said with determination. "I'll see you tomorrow."

"Yeah." I hung up and stared into the darkness for a long time before falling asleep.

So far, Lou and I had only had two dates. Since both Ter and Scott worked Monday nights, we tried for a third date the following Monday. I'd found a note from Lou in my locker saying he'd pick me up at six at our usual drop-off point a block away from my house.

As I waited for Lou, I wondered how many

more dates we would have before we figured out what to do about Scott and Ter. So far, neither Lou nor I had expressed how we felt about each other. I hadn't told him that I loved him, and he hadn't told me that he loved me. I was pretty sure I loved him. Did he love me?

I resisted the urge to rip out one of the neighbor's shasta daisies and perform the he-loves-me-he-loves-me-not ritual on it. I was afraid to face the answer. Because no matter how it turned out, somebody was going to get hurt.

Lou arrived on time, and we began discussing how we would spend the evening. There weren't any movies we were interested in. It was too chilly for the beach. And we couldn't go to any of the malls because someone might recognize us. Then Lou mentioned that there was an art exhibit by Chicanos going on at Cal Poly, the local college, so we decided to drive up there to see it. I found it interesting, especially with Lou's explanations of the different photographs and sculptures. And I was already familiar with some of Chicano history, because I had picked up a lot from Ter over the years.

Lou and I came across a painting depicting several members of a gang. They stood on a street corner, wearing baggy pants and sullen expressions. "This is an example of what my father was trying to get us away from when we moved up here from the barrio—" Lou suddenly stopped speaking, and his grip on my hand tightened.

Then I heard a girl's voice behind me. "Hi, you two," she said.

I turned around and saw Cathy and Kevin. I had known that Kevin was interested in Cathy, but I hadn't known they were actually dating. Of course, I'd been so obsessed with my own life lately, it wasn't surprising I'd lost touch with other people.

Lou dropped my hand, and I inched away from him, but I'm sure Cathy and Kevin had already seen us holding hands and standing close together.

"Hi," I said, trying to sound normal. Cathy looked at me with a questioning expression. "I didn't know you guys were interested in art," I said to them.

"We were going to see a movie, but there's nothing good in the theaters," Kevin explained. His expression gave away nothing of his thoughts, but I was sure he was curious about what Lou and I were doing together.

"And since we have so many Chicanos in the area," Cathy went on with a shy glance at Lou, "I suggested we come see the exhibit."

"Oh," I said, feeling awkward and self-conscious.

"Well, we're about done here and we have to get going," Lou said suddenly. "See you."

We left quickly and headed straight for his truck without saying a word. Lou started driving back toward Pismo, and I watched the road silently. I noticed he didn't take a direct route home. Instead he took the long way, passing farms and vineyards. In the dusk the distant mountains looked blue and misty.

After several minutes, Lou spoke. "We have to talk about this," he said.

I nodded. "I know." My voice came out choked, and I sounded as if I were on the verge of tears.

Lou drove a little farther, then turned off on a side road that led up into the hills, past horse ranches. There was a winery on top of a small hill, and its parking lot was empty. Lou pulled in and parked in a spot overlooking miles and miles of rolling hills.

"We can't go on like this," Lou said, turning to look at me. "We have to make some kind of decision."

"I know," I answered, looking down into my lap.

"So, do we tell Scott and Ter about us? Or . . ." He paused, then said the words I dreaded. "Or give each other up?"

I shivered at the thought of losing him. But I

knew he was right. We had to make a decision. The constant tension caused by our sneaking around was becoming impossible to bear. "If we tell Scott and Ter—" I began.

"We lose our best friends," Lou said, finishing my sentence.

I swallowed back an obstruction in my throat. My eyes burned. My head ached. Ter had never done anything to hurt me. To hurt *her* after all our years of friendship seemed too awful to contemplate.

Lou shifted in his seat. "Well, I guess if we're not in, uh, love with each other yet, we could go back to the way we were." If Lou loved me, this would have been the time for him to say so. But he hadn't. He had spoken slowly and deliberately as if he didn't like telling me that he hadn't fallen in love with me the way he'd thought he might.

I closed my eyes. A dull ache seemed to be filling my whole body. At that moment, I knew I loved him, but I wasn't brave enough to put my heart out in full view and tell him so.

"Yeah" was all I could get past the lump in my throat.

Lou didn't say anything. He just stared straight ahead, his body upright and rigid. Finally he reached for the ignition and started the truck.

"That's it then," he said in a strained voice. "I guess you can go on dating Scott, and I'll—" He didn't finish the thought, but I guessed he was trying to tell me that he'd go on dating Ter. I was happy for her. But I wanted to die.

We drove in total silence back to my neighborhood. For the last time Lou parked down the road from my house. He turned toward me, but I couldn't see his face in the darkness. He probably couldn't see mine either, and I was thankful for that. Tears burned my eyes, and I knew they would start falling any second.

"Well, that's that, I guess," Lou said.

"Yeah."

"See you tomorrow."

"Umhm."

Lou put his hands on the steering wheel.

He can't wait for me to get out of here, I thought. I jumped out of the truck, slammed the door shut behind me, and raced home.

fourteen

I lived through the next week feeling as if someone had shot my brain full of Novocain. I went through every school day looking like a model student, appearing attentive to the teachers in class. I sat up straight at my desk and looked directly ahead of me, my focus never wavering. But I had no idea what my teachers were saying.

My mother complained that we never had time for our cooking lessons because I was always practicing for the band, and when I was home I was practicing my violin. She was right. I had gone over the score for *The Nutcracker* so much, I was beginning to hate it. But playing music I hated was far better than being alone with my thoughts.

I managed to get through the band's practice sessions by concentrating on my music to the exclusion of everything else. I started to play really well as a result, and Scott noticed the improvement.

"Krista, you're really turning into a great musician," he said to me one day.

"Thanks," I said and forced a smile.

"I knew you had it in you the first time I heard you play," he went on. He nodded his head toward Lou and Ter. "If these two ever quit, you and I can make a career together."

"Hey, wait a minute," Ter objected. "Don't write us off so quickly."

He grinned at her. "Well, I guess you're not a bad musician, either," he said. "But Lou, there, seems to be in a trance these days."

Lou looked over at us and shrugged.

"What do you mean?" Ter asked, rising to Lou's defense.

"Oh, nothing," Scott said. "I was just kidding." He bent over his amp and began fiddling with some dials.

But I knew Scott wasn't kidding. Lou had been doing a decent job of playing the drums, but he did lack zip. I wondered if he was sorry he'd broken up with me. Or was he just tired of being with Ter? Or was it possible that he didn't want to be with the band anymore?

I'd been careful not to bring up Lou in conversations I had with Ter. And oddly, she hadn't said anything about him either. It wasn't like Ter to keep her thoughts to herself, and it was odd that she had suddenly stopped talking to me about him. I wondered for one horrible moment if Cathy and Kevin had told her they'd seen us at the exhibit. But I knew Ter would've just asked me about it if she had heard something. She would never suspect any wrongdoing.

Scott came by work one Sunday night, and hung around until I got off work at ten.

"My parents have agreed to let me major in music at the college of my choice," he announced jubilantly when I joined him outside the restaurant.

"That's great," I said, truly happy for him.

"You know what this means?" he asked, smiling.

"No. What?"

"You and I should pick the same college."

"Huh? Why?" I asked.

He gave me a look that told me he thought the reasons were obvious. "Because if we're going to keep playing together, you and I have to go to the same college."

I tried to think of an answer that wouldn't seem too insensitive. Finally I just gave up and said honestly, "Scott, what about my career as a storyteller?"

He frowned. "Krista, you won't have to do that if we can make a career together," he said. "I guess you're not as gung ho about being a musician as I thought."

"But, Scott, I told you. I really want to be a storyteller," I said. "And I've already chosen the colleges I'm going to apply to. I'm majoring in English, remember? So I can be a teacher?" I tried to make eye contact with him as I spoke, but he was looking down at the pavement.

He ran a hand through his hair, then gave me a searching look. "But if we make it, you won't ever have to teach English," he said. "Besides, you could use the connections you'd have in the music business to get storytelling jobs."

I bit my lip, knowing that I couldn't let him go on thinking that I shared his dreams. "Scott, I'm sorry," I said. "But as much as playing in the band has been a dream come true, music is not the most important aspect of my life. You've wanted to be a musician for years. I just wanted to have fun with music—not make it my whole life." I looked at him, hoping he'd understand.

He swallowed, and then sighed. "I guess I'm

stupid to expect you to become a part of my dreams, huh?"

I touched his arm. "Scott, you can still be a musician even if I don't want to make a career of it. You have all the talent anyway."

"That's not true," Scott objected. But then a smile spread across his face. "You really think I'm talented?"

"Yes," I said sincerely. And it was true. Scott probably had the skill to go on to be a professional musician. I was pretty good, too, but I knew I wasn't in his league.

Somehow I got through the next week. I had finally saved enough money to get my car fixed, so that made me feel pretty good. I told Ter that she should let me drive her around for a while in exchange for all the times she'd picked me up and taken me home, and she said something strange in response: "I'm not sure I'll feel safe being driven by someone who acts as if an alien has taken over her body."

"What do you mean?" I said, confused. We were talking on the phone, and I wished that I could see her face.

"I mean, you haven't been you lately," she said. "Sometimes I look at you and you have this weird expression on your face, as if you're just a little bit crazy." She paused, and then said in a gentle voice that almost tore my heart out, "Is something wrong between you and Scott? You know I love you more than anyone, and if you need to talk about it, I'm here."

"I know," I choked out. "But really, Ter, there's nothing to talk about."

Two weeks had passed since Lou and I broke up. We had both managed to get through the times we practiced with the band—but we didn't look at each other much during the sessions. Scott had been rehearsing us like crazy for the next gig, so we hadn't had any time for much more than our music. And there were no opportunities for the four of us to go out. So that helped. But it was getting harder for me to pretend Lou wasn't in the band room during orchestra, or behind me in the garage during our sessions.

I continued to work at Taco Bell, but I was growing more and more weary of the job. I began waiting on people as if I were in a trance, and I walked around like a tired old woman. Then, one night, I spotted Lou waiting in line behind a customer I was serving.

"Lou!" I exclaimed.

He waved and gave me a half smile.

Quickly I served the customer, and Lou stepped forward, looking around anxiously. "Uh,

I knew you worked tonight so I decided to drop by," he said. "I have to talk to you. I, uh, can't stand not being with you anymore."

The heaviness that had weighed me down suddenly lifted. "Oh, Lou!" I said. "I want to talk to you, too. But when?"

"I'm on my way to work right now," he said. "And I have to work right after school tomorrow, but I get off at seven. So can you meet me at the library tomorrow night around seven fifteen?" He grinned. "Our usual aisle?"

I nodded vigorously.

"Great. See you then," he said. He smiled, then turned and left the restaurant.

Lou missed me! It had to mean he cared! I thought as I scurried around Taco Bell, serving customers at breakneck speed. It was strange that he picked the library as our meeting place, but maybe he thought it was the safest place to meet. If anyone we knew saw us there, they'd think we were just studying.

I was in the library the next night at exactly seven. Lou came in fifteen minutes later. I rose from the table where I'd been waiting and strolled toward the aisle. I was beginning to develop affection for that aisle. Wonderful things always happened when I was in it. Soon I'd even stop complaining about economics, I thought, laughing.

Lou rounded the corner and walked up to me, enfolding me in his arms. "Krista," he whispered in my ear. "The last couple of weeks have been awful. Every time I was near you, I would go out of my mind. I can't take it anymore."

I hugged him. Mixed emotions clogged my throat, making it impossible for me to speak at first. But finally I managed. "I can't take it anymore either," I said.

Lou took my hand, and we left the library. We sat in his truck and kissed until neither of us could breathe anymore.

Then he took a deep breath and leaned back in his seat. "Even if you don't feel the same way about me, I have to tell you something," he said, looking at me. "Krista, I . . . I think I've fallen in love with you."

"Then why did you send me away?" I asked, confused. "Why did you go back to Ter?"

"I didn't go back to Ter," he said. "I haven't exactly ended things with her, but I haven't spent any time alone with her either." He took my hand. "And Krista, I never sent you away."

"Yes, you did," I insisted. "That night at the winery you said that if we weren't in love with each other—'"

"But you didn't argue!" Lou blurted out. "I figured if you *did* love me, you'd have said so right then. But when you didn't, I assumed your feelings for me weren't that strong. At least not strong enough to want to break up our friendships with Ter and Scott."

I listened to his explanation, struggling to make sense of it all. I shook my head in disbelief. I had misinterpreted everything he had said that night at the winery.

"And let's face it," he went on. "If we tell them, it's going to mean the end of our friendships. I mean, Scott's wild about you. If I take you away from him, he'll never forgive me." He paused and leaned in closer to me. "Krista, how do you feel about Scott?"

"Don't you know?" I asked incredulously. I kissed him hard. "Can't you tell what I want? I don't want Scott." I bit my lip before going on. "Lou, I love you."

Lou took a deep breath. "Man, what a waste!" he said, raising his hands to his head. "All this misery just because I didn't know how you felt. Talk about stupid."

I smiled at him. "Well, that's all over now."

"Yeah." He frowned and looked at me. "Now we gotta tell Scott and Teresa. And who knows? Maybe they'll understand." He shook his head doubtfully. "We just have to tell them that we want to be with each other. And maybe they'll want what's best for us. Right?"

"I don't know, Lou," I said honestly. "If things

were reversed, how would we react?"

We looked at each other and knew the answer. It was going to be an awful scene.

We decided to break the news to Scott and Ter at our practice session right after school the next day. As soon as we got to Lou's garage, I positioned myself right beside Lou.

"We have something we'd like to talk about before we, uh, play," Lou said, facing Scott and Ter.

My stomach heaved, my fingers were ice cold, and I thought my legs were going to give out under me.

"What is it?" Scott asked, looking puzzled.

Lou shifted on his feet and glanced at me briefly. "First I want to say that Krista and I really care for you guys," he began.

I saw Scott's and Ter's reaction to hearing Lou say, "Krista and I." Scott had suddenly stood stock still. Ter's face paled, and her eyes danced from me to Lou, as if she were afraid to look at either one of us.

"We would never deliberately do anything to hurt you," Lou went on. "And we both know what we're about to tell you might do that." He paused, and I saw a muscle jump in his jaw. Then he glanced at me, and I tried to send him an encouraging look. "Krista and I have discovered that we care for each other and we want to date each other."

Ter gasped.

"You mean, you and Krista instead of me and Krista?" Scott said, sounding confused.

"So that's why you've been acting so funny!" Ter exclaimed, looking at me. Then her eyes settled on Lou, and she looked at him with warmth and sadness.

"Oh, Ter!" I said, lurching forward. "I didn't want this to happen. I fought it. You have to believe me." I stood in front of her, my eyes begging her to understand.

She shook her head. "And all this time I thought maybe you weren't getting along with Scott," she said in a tight voice. "I *never* would've thought you were after Lou."

I moved toward her, but she backed away from me. Shaking her head, she continued backing up until she reached the open garage door. She looked at Lou. "And I really thought you were different from the other guys," she spat out at him. Then her expression changed, and she appeared deeply injured. "I guess you are different, but you still don't want me." She stood there, looking like a lost child.

Lou looked helpless. "I'm sorry, I just—" He lowered his eyes, unable to go on. Then he added lamely, "You really are a special person,

Teresa. But I guess that wasn't enough to make things work between us. The more I was around Krista, the more I realized that I really liked her."

"Just when did you two decide all this?" Scott said, his tone biting.

"Well, uh, a couple of weeks ago," Lou said in a low voice. "More like three or four."

"What?" Scott said. He shook his head as if he didn't trust his hearing. Then he switched his gaze to me. He opened his mouth, but no sound came out.

"Krista and I were seeing each other for a couple of weeks without telling you guys," Lou confessed, "just to see if we really did like each other." He spoke hurriedly, as if he needed to get the story out fast. "Then we decided we couldn't hurt you guys, so we tried to go back to having things the way they were. But it didn't work. We really care about each other."

Scott started pacing around the garage. "So what about the band?" he asked. "I mean, will we keep playing?"

"No, I couldn't!" Ter shouted.

Scott raised his eyebrows and looked at her. "What do you mean, you couldn't? Doesn't the band *mean* anything to you?"

Ter just shook her head, staring first at me, then at Lou.

"But we just got ourselves some gigs," Scott

said almost desperately. "We're starting to earn money. What am I supposed to tell that guy from the condos?"

"Maybe we can still play," I heard myself suggest. Right. And maybe we could all sign a suicide pact, I thought. It wouldn't hurt any less.

"I don't know if it would work," Lou said, looking at Ter.

"Oh, come on," Scott insisted. "This band is more important than our personal lives. It wouldn't be the first time romances in a band regrouped. That happens all the time. Are we going destroy a great band just because our love lives didn't work out the way we wanted?" He was looking at Ter, almost begging her.

I realized then how far Scott would go to follow his dreams. Music came before everything else in his life. And even though I didn't want to be with Scott, I couldn't help but feel hurt that he seemed more upset about the band dissolving than about our relationship ending. Then I chastised myself. Maybe it *was* better if we kept the band going. It wasn't that important to me, but if Lou wanted to give it a try, I would too.

I walked over to Scott. "I guess I could keep playing," I said.

"Well, I won't!" Ter yelled. She glared at Scott.

213

"There are more important things than playing a couple of guitars. Things like loyalty!" She shot me a piercing look. "I can't believe you would do this, Krista. You knew how much I cared for Lou." Tears were beginning to stream down her cheeks. She swallowed, then said in a voice filled with torment, "I don't want to be your friend anymore—not if you can do something like this!" She stifled a cry, then spun around and ran to her car.

"Wait!" Scott called and raced after her. It should have been me who ran after her, but I felt as if my feet were encased in blocks of ice.

Lou took my hand and held it. But the warmth of his hand gave me little comfort.

Scott came back into the garage. "Teresa's really hurting," he said. "I sure hope it's all worth it." He turned his back to us and started to collect his instruments.

Lou and I watched as he packed up his things. After he was through, he looked at me. "Teresa's not the only one who got hurt."

I opened my mouth to say something, but the words wouldn't come. What could I possibly say?

Scott loaded up in his Jeep and drove away, and I collapsed in Lou's arms, my body wracked with soul-deep tears.

fifteen

Life without Ter was awful. Having her around was something I had gotten so used to. Now that she was gone, I felt as if someone close to me had died. I drove to school alone everyday. There was no one to share thoughts with on the way. And there were no more telephone calls from her after dinner. I missed her terribly.

Without band practice, Lou and I had more time to spend together. But still, we were miserable.

"Scott doesn't even talk to me," Lou said the week following the big scene. "Except maybe to answer my questions with one word. I have to phrase my questions so that they only require a yes or no in response."

We were parked at Morro Bay, sitting in his truck and staring out to sea. Our fingers were locked together, and Lou had an arm slung over my shoulders.

"Ter's worse," I told him. "She sees me coming down the hall and turns away. She makes sure she's never at her locker when I'm at mine. And orchestra is horrible. It's so hard to sit next to someone who won't look at you, or talk to you."

"Scott's not that bad," he said.

"Has he said anything about the gig?" I asked.

"He just said he'd handle it, that's all." Lou dug in his pants pocket and handed me a clipping from a newspaper. "Read this," he said.

"Band members wanted," I said, reading out loud. "Lead guitarist and keyboardist need drummer and base guitarist. Gigs booked. Need players quick."

"That phone number's Scott's," Lou said. "You know what that means?"

"Yeah, I guess he convinced Ter to play. I didn't know." I folded up the ad, then looked at Lou. "Are you sorry?" I knew he didn't need me to explain what I was asking. I had asked myself the same question over and over again. Was our relationship worth losing our best friends?

"No," he said firmly. Then he hugged me closer. "I love you, Krista. Those two will come around. Just give them time." His words were reassuring, but his tone lacked the conviction I wanted to hear.

Cathy called me on the phone a week after the big blow out to find out what the story was. Rumors had been flying all over school. I explained the whole situation to her as best I could.

"What a mess," she said. "And everyone in school thought it was so neat about you guys." She paused. "But you know, Krista. You and Ter go way back. That's got to be good for something. Maybe if I talk to her—"

"No!" I cried. I didn't want Ter to think I was talking behind her back. "Just keep this between you and me," I told Cathy.

"Well, okay," Cathy agreed reluctantly.

Lou and I were really upset about losing Scott and Ter, and we talked about it constantly. But I don't think either one of us realized just how depressed we were, until one Monday night, two weeks after the band split up.

Lou and I were in his truck, heading for Pismo Beach to catch the sunset. The air was clear, and there had been a breeze all day that had blown the fog out. It was pretty warm for an October night, and I was feeling particularly blue. So Lou thought watching the sunset might cheer me up.

We were driving down Grande Avenue, approaching the entrance to the beach, and I was crying. Lou kept trying to reason with me, but nothing he said made me feel any better.

"Krista, I really think we have to put this whole mess behind us, and get on with *us*," he told me.

"Well maybe you can do that, but I can't!"

Lou sighed. "I'm not saying it's going to be easy."

"It's impossible," I said. "My friendship with Ter goes so far back. I almost don't know who I am without her."

"Well, my friendship with Scott goes way back too," he said, sounding slightly annoyed.

"If you think it's possible to put this behind us, then obviously guys don't have the same kind of relationships girls do," I said angrily.

"Oh, really?" Lou said, his voice rising. "Where did you get *that* idea?"

I'd never heard Lou use that tone of voice before, and I felt as if I'd just been slapped. I was about to apologize, but he went on.

"Get this straight," he said fiercely. "My friendship with Scott is just as important to me as yours is with Teresa." He slammed a fist on the steering wheel, and I jerked back, frightened. "I suppose you think guys are supposed to be these macho types without any feelings. Well maybe we don't show them like you girls, but we sure do have—"

"Look out!" I screamed.

A tiny dog had dashed out into the street, chasing a ball. Some kids nearby had their mouths open, but I couldn't hear their screaming. Lou wrenched the wheel instinctively, and we crossed over to the oncoming lane.

I remember seeing the big panel truck coming at us and the look on the driver's face. I remember how it felt when Lou slammed on the brakes. The seat belt cut into my body, and I heard the sound of metal crunching and glass shattering. I remember thinking a ridiculous thought: We're going to miss the sunset.

And that's all I remember.

We were told that the driver of the panel truck had only minor injuries and was released from the hospital almost immediately. Lou's truck took a beating, though. And so did we. I woke up in our community hospital, feeling sore all over. Bandages seemed to cover most of my body: my chest, my arms, my head. I stared up at the ceiling, afraid to move. What happened? I wondered. The door to the hallway was open, and I could hear voices. Then my mother and father came in.

"Krista!" they cried in unison, smiles lighting up their faces.

They kissed me and did everything they could to make me feel more comfortable. Afterward they told me I'd suffered a concussion, fractured two ribs, and was covered with glass cuts. Lou was in a room down the hall. His left ankle was broken. And like me, he had glass cuts all over his face and arms. We were both badly bruised. But, miraculously, that was all of our injuries.

"Thank God you were wearing seat belts," my mother said. "We were so worried."

My father was holding my hand as if he thought I'd be taken away from him. "You've been unconscious for almost a whole day," he told me.

"Can I see Lou?" I asked. My parents hadn't known that I was seeing Lou, and I knew I would have to tell them the whole story later on. But for now, they seemed too worried about my health to wonder why I had been with him instead of Scott.

Mom smiled. "Well, we'll let the doctor know you're awake, and he can decide."

I wanted to see Lou so badly that it hurt me more than my injuries. And I wondered if Scott and Ter had heard about the accident. Had they already come to see us?

My parents came back to report that the doctor would be in to see me later. They stayed with me a while longer, but I was too tired to hold a conversation, so they left just before dinner. Finally the doctor came in with a wheel-chair and told me I could see Lou. He buzzed for a nurse, then they both helped me into the chair and wheeled me out of my room.

Lou looked awful. His face was crisscrossed with scratches, and there were small bandages down his left cheek. His leg was bound by a cast from foot to knee.

"Lou," I said.

His eyes flickered open, and he reached for me. "Krista."

We held hands for a while without speaking. After a moment, I cleared my throat. "Do you think they know?" I asked.

"I don't know," he answered. "Did you ask your parents?"

"No. I guess I was afraid to."

He nodded. "Yeah, I know what you mean. I didn't ask mine either. They were here just a minute ago."

Again we were silent. Then I said, "I think they would want to see us. I mean, even if they're mad at us . . . we've known each other so long."

Lou squeezed my hand. "Krista," he said hoarsely. "Don't worry. They'll show up."

"Yeah." I let go of Lou's hand and leaned back in my chair. A wave of exhaustion had washed over me, and I was about to go back to my room. Then there was a knock at the door.

"Come in," Lou said as loudly as he could.

The door opened, and Scott and Ter came in.

I smiled at them, and Lou cried out, "Amigo!"

Ter came in first, though hesitantly, and Scott followed right behind her.

"Hi," Scott said to me, but his eyes didn't quite meet mine.

Ter came over beside me. "Hi, Krista," she said softly. "How are you feeling?"

"I'm okay. Thanks," I said, smiling at her. I heard warmth in her voice, and I ached to hug her, but she was standing a few feet away from me, looking around the room restlessly.

"You guys got the whole school stirred up," Scott said.

"Yeah, you should hear everyone," Ter added. "It's all everyone's talking about."

Scott looked at Lou's cast and grinned. "Man, look at all that white space just waiting to be filled."

"Yeah," Lou said, smiling.

"Well, at least you can still beat your drums," Scott said. "Your arms seem to be okay. Remember Ricky Travis? When he broke his ankle in a football game, he still managed to move his whole leg up and down so he could work the pedal."

222

"That's right," Lou said, lifting his left leg experimentally. "I guess I can do the same thing."

The guys seemed to be doing better at getting back on their old footing than Ter and me. Her eyes were dancing all over the room, as if she were afraid to look too closely at either me or Lou. And then she burst out suddenly. "I couldn't believe it when your mom called me last night. She said you'd been in a terrible accident, and you were unconscious." Her eyes met mine, and I knew that she still cared.

"Yeah? She didn't tell me she called you," I said.

"It was at about ten last night. So today's the first we could come see you." Ter was rambling on nervously.

"Oh."

"Does your head hurt?" she asked. "I asked Cathy, whose aunt is a nurse, about concussions, and she said they can cause terrible headaches."

"Yeah, my head does hurt a little," I said. "Especially if I move it too suddenly."

"Um, I put something in your room," she said, looking at her feet.

"Yeah? What is it?"

"It's something I made at work," she said. "You'll see it when you get back there."

"Oh, okay. Thanks," I said.

A nurse bustled in to check Lou's temperature,

his pulse, and his cast. Then she bustled out again.

"Why do they want my temperature," Lou grumbled. "I'm maimed, not sick."

"They gotta earn their keep, I guess," Scott joked. Lou chuckled, then another awkward silence descended on us.

God, this is awful, I thought. We can't even hold a decent conversation with our best friends anymore.

"So," Lou said. "Did you guys get any answers to your ad?"

Scott turned to him, looking surprised. "You saw it?"

Lou nodded.

"Well, yeah, we had a couple of kids come over and audition, but compared to you two, they were amateurs." He started pacing around the room as he spoke. "You know, you two were half of what made our band what it was. That guy from the condos liked the sound all four of us made together." He shot Ter a look. "Teresa and I were talking. We think maybe we should try playing that gig in two weeks." He stopped pacing and looked at us. "If you guys are out by then, and if your injuries don't keep you from playing, would you perform one last time?"

Lou shifted in his bed as if he were lying on

rocks, and I averted Ter's eyes. I wanted to play in the band again, and I was sure Lou did too, but the dynamics of the band wouldn't be the same. And I thought it might be painful for Ter and Scott to see Lou and I me as a couple.

"We'll have to check with our doctors," Lou said.

"Yeah, of course," Scott agreed quickly. "Listen, you don't have to tell us right now. Talk about it first. Let us know when you guys are ready. You might even think about joining up with us again permanently."

"Yeah, okay," Lou said, looking at me.

"Well, I guess we should let you guys rest now," Scott said. "We'll come visit again."

Ter sprang to her feet from the chair she was sitting in. "Yeah, you guys must be tired," she said.

After Scott and Ter left, Lou and I talked for a few minutes about joining up with the band again. We decided that we'd wait and see what the doctors had to say, then take it from there.

I buzzed for the nurse, and she came in to wheel me back to my room. As soon as I got there I saw the beautiful silk flower arrangement Ter had left for me and burst into tears.

"Oh, I'll bet you're feeling miserable," the nurse said, misinterpreting my tears. "I'll go get the doctor." She helped me into bed, and hurried out of the room.

I reached out and touched the petal of a pink rose. Ter had put together the arrangement, using colors that would match my room at home. She was so thoughtful. And yet when we were all in Lou's room, she had kept her distance from me. I wondered if I could bear playing in the band, knowing that things would never be the same with her again.

Both Scott and Ter worked the next day, so we didn't see them, but they each called to see how we were. Over the phone, Ter seemed so much more at ease with me, and I began to feel more optimistic about rebuilding our friendship. She laughed and joked around just as she used to, and it was almost as if nothing had happened between us.

And in my conversation with Scott, we managed to clear the air between us. "You know," he said halfway into our chat, "I was really upset about you and Lou—"

"I'm so sorry, Scott," I said.

"Wait. I, uh, have to admit though that I came to realize that I'd kind of looked at you as a band member first and a girlfriend second," he said. "After I had lots of time to think about it, I realized that you and Lou had a lot more in common than you and I did. You guys just seemed to think alike." He chuckled. "So, anyway, I really hope you two decide to play with us for that gig."

"Thanks, Scott," I said. "Thanks for being so understanding."

After I told Lou what Scott had said, he was quiet for a moment. Then he said, "See why I love that guy?"

We were released the following day. Our doctor told us that he saw no reason why we couldn't play our instruments. He said our bodies would tell us what we could and couldn't do, and he didn't seem particularly worried about us hurting ourselves.

We decided we'd tell Scott and Ter that we wanted to play the gig and rejoin the band. The tension between Ter and me seemed to have disappeared, and I thought that our friendship would soon be back to normal again. Lou felt the same way about his friendship with Scott, so after discussing things, we both decided that we wanted to be a part of the band again.

It was close to the end of the school day when we were released from the hospital. Lou and I had arranged for my father to come pick us up and drive us over to the school so that we could tell Scott and Ter the good news in person. When my father pulled up in front of the school, we spotted Ter's car and Scott's Jeep in the student parking lot. My father helped us out of his car, and I told him we'd get a ride home from Scott. He drove away, leaving Lou and I right next to Ter's car. Then the final bell rang, and kids began pouring out of the class-rooms.

I looked at Lou and reached out for his hand. "You're sure this is what you want?"

Lou nodded. "Yeah, I am."

Soon Ter and Scott came out of the main building, talking to each other. They came a little closer to us, but neither of them seemed to notice us. Then Scott began to veer off to his Jeep, and Ter saw us leaning against her car. I saw her mouth drop open, then Scott followed her line of vision, and his eyes widened when he spotted us.

Ter immediately dashed forward. "Krista! Lou! You got out!" Her eyes were brimming with tears, and her mouth turned up at the corners in a tremulous smile.

Then Scott ran up to us, grabbed Lou's hand, and pumped it up and down. "It's great to see you up and around, amigo. I can't believe you guys got out so quickly. The way you two looked the other day, Ter and I thought you were going to be there for days." He laughed and slapped Lou lightly on the shoulder. "We were afraid you might not feel good enough to play that gig coming up."

"Really?" I said, looking at Ter.

She nodded. "We thought we were going to have to settle for two amateur musicians for the gig—" She covered her mouth with a hand and threw a glance at Scott who was looking at us closely. "Um, did you decide?" she said hesitantly. "About playing the gig?"

I looked at Lou.

"Yes," Lou said. "We want to play it *and* rejoin the band."

"Great!" Scott said, raising a fist into the air. "High Pressure's back in business."

Ter smiled. "This is perfect! Now I won't have to get used to two new people," she said.

I looked at Ter and felt the urge to throw my arms around her. But instead, I leaned toward her, holding my arms open, and she leaped forward and hugged me fiercely.

"I'm so sorry," I whispered.

"Me too," she cried. "Oh, I've missed you!"

Tears started to well up in my eyes, and I hugged her even closer.

"These last few weeks have been horrible," she said. "I couldn't stand not being your friend, even if you did get the guy I wanted. Our friendship was the most important thing in the world to me."

"Oh, Ter!" I cried. "Things were awful for me, too. Everywhere I looked reminded me of you." I pulled back, smiled through my tears, and said, *Beaches*.

"Yes!" Ter said, squealing.

I was bursting with happiness. Ter was ready to forgive me and take me back as her friend. And though I knew it would take time to rebuild her trust in me, we were definitely on our way to becoming best friends again. I wanted to shout and jump around in the parking lot, but my body hurt too much. So I just hugged Ter harder.

Look for Beverly Hills, 90210 — the ONLY authorized novels around!

Spelling Ent. Inc.

Beverly Hills, 90210
Beverly Hills, 90210:
Exposed!
Beverly Hills, 90210:
No Secrets
Beverly Hills, 90210:
Which Way to the Beach
Beverly Hills, 90210:
Fantasies
Beverly Hills, 90210:
'Tis the Season

Available at bookstores now!

🔲 HarperPaperbacks
A Division of HarperCollinsPublishers

bh 1